On A Midnight Clear
An Adam Fraley Mystery

Henry Hoffman

Published by
Melange Books, LLC
White Bear Lake, MN 55110
www.melange-books.com

On A Midnight Clear ~ Copyright © 2016 by Henry Hoffman

ISBN: 978-1-68046-292-0 Print

Cover Art by Stephanie Flint

For where your treasure is,
there also will your heart be.
--Luke 12:34

CHAPTER ONE

December 24, 1991

Crossing the Kansas border into Colorado on an arrow-straight strip of interstate in his new Ford pickup, Adam Fraley came to realize the grand vision he believed awaited him down the road was not to be.

He recalled the first time he made the same overland journey from his hometown of Tampa, Florida five years earlier. It was then he discovered Eastern Colorado had much in common with Western Kansas—endless flatland stretching to the horizon, intersected by a highway offering random views of wind turbines, grazing cattle, occasional gas stations and not much else. Still, if he recollected right, in less than an hour from having crossed the border what appeared to be a line of towering thunderheads came suddenly into view on the distant horizon. On second glance, they turned out to be towering peaks, a jagged wall of wonder representing the front range of the Rockies' eastern slopes.

On this occasion, there would be no mile-high apparition to behold, no spectacle to relieve the boredom of the all too familiar landscape. The standard "welcome-to-our-state" roadside sign would have to suffice thanks to an overcast sky that limited visibility. A few miles further down the road light snow flakes began to flitter in the chilly air, dancing off his windshield in an aimless manner, raising the possibility of another grand vision awaiting him—that of a white Christmas. He had checked on the weather prior to departure. Light snow was in the forecast but nothing much more. In addition, he had timed his trip to arrive in Colorado Springs by early evening. A former Air Force buddy by the name of Reggie Fielding was expecting him. It was a holiday getaway. His parents were going on a Christmas cruise, so he decided to accept Reggie's invitation to spend the holidays in the mountains. Perhaps he could also lift his old colleague's spirits, which had taken a nosedive as the result of losing a lucrative job. Going from head of corporate security at an industrial firm to part-time bartender was enough to dim anyone's holiday spirits. The reason for his dismissal was yet unknown but if Adam had to guess, it was Reggie's almost reflex action to question a manager's decision. It was second nature for him to take the other side of an argument to the point of insubordination, if not outright confrontation. "You should have started up your own private investigation firm," he'd told him, leaving out the "like I did with Adam Fraley Private Investigations." If anyone was cut out to be his own boss, it was Reggie.

Reaching the small town of Limon, some 70 miles beyond the Kansas border, Adam switched from the Interstate 70 to Highway 24, which would lead him in a more southwesterly direction for the remainder of the way to the juncture of I-25 and Colorado Springs. Ten miles west of Limon the snow increased in intensity. He punched on the pickup's radio and despite heavy static found a Denver station broadcasting those worrisome words—travelers' warning. The weather bureau had issued a revised forecast calling for heavy snow throughout the region. He checked the dashboard clock—6:10 p.m. The sun had disappeared hours ago leaving the road a swirl of headlights and blowing snow. Traffic was thinning as more motorists decided to abandon the highway due to the worsening conditions. An hour out of Colorado Springs, the accumulation of snow on the road made it nearly indistinct. The fact he had four-wheel drive did little to ease his concern. A wise decision would have been for him to find a place to spend the night, but he was the sort to get where he was going once on the move.

Under near whiteout conditions and unable to distinguish the road markings, he slowed his truck to a crawl. Only an isolated motorist or two could be seen braving the conditions. Ahead of him loomed the back of a truck, large enough to be an eighteen-wheeler, its bright taillights inviting him to follow in its tracks. He could not be more than 25 miles from Interstate 25, the highway paralleling the eastern slopes. Once there he could find a motel and call Reggie to let him know of his plight.

For nearly an hour, Adam's gaze locked onto the truck's burning rear orbs, settling him into a near hypnotic state. Eventually jarring him to his senses was the sudden flashing of the truck's right turn signal. He looked for signs of civilization. Were they approaching I-25? From the lay of the land and lack of traffic, it appeared not. A roadside sign, its message blurred by snow blowing horizontal, indicated the truck was exiting onto a county road. Adam decided to follow in his tracks, believing the truck was his sole hope of reaching a safe landing zone, be it a truck stop or major traffic route with lodging nearby. The trailing lasted another half hour, when the truck's turn light again flashed and the vehicle eased onto the shoulder of the road. The reason for the exit immediately became clear. The trucker was packing it in for the night, deciding to wait it out in the warmth of his cab. Adam slid his pickup onto the shoulder in front of the trucker, debating whether to call it a night as well. The debate ended when the trucker flashed his high beams on, saying, in effect, this was his territory.

Adam motored on, determined to reach his destination. Ruts left in the snow pack by earlier trailblazers now served as his guide. A while longer and with no warning the ghostly overhead lights of Interstate 25 appeared above him, as if arising out of a fog bank. He drove through an underpass on a snow-packed road offering no on or off ramps, at least none that were visible. He had passed the point of no return. Somewhere ahead he was bound to hit a wall of mountains. At the pace he was traveling, it would hardly leave a dent, he mused. All kidding aside, it was time for him to humble himself and seek out the first human to confess he was lost.

Little by little, Adam became aware of a transformation in the land, despite his view being limited to the reach of his headlights. He was gaining altitude, heading up a rise closely bordered by thickets of pine trees, their branches sagging from the weight of the snow piled atop them. Unfortunately, civilization appeared non-existent on the pathway he was pursuing. That was until he approached the second crest of what turned out to be a series of rises. Coming off the crest in the opposite direction was a motorist rollicking along with his high beams ablaze. Adam swerved to avoid the driver, thereby managing to escape a collision. "At least someone knows where he's going," he muttered, glancing back at the disappearing driver.

Coming off a third crest, Adam spotted a flood of light filtering through the pines off to his right. At the bottom of the hill appeared a clearing in the woods. Planted in the middle of the field, a sizable log cabin sat decked out in Christmas finery. Reaching the base of the incline, he eased his pickup to the side of the road, shutting it down to take in the sight. The stillness surrounding him was a welcome relief from the harried atmosphere of the open road he had battled through for the past several hours. The wind had subsided, though the snow continued to fall soft and untouched, blanketing the landscape with a thick white carpet.

Adam turned his attention to the cabin and its environs, spread before him like the December cover of a country living magazine. Not only was the cabin outlined in lights, nearby trees had also received the decorative treatment. The glow cast over the clearing by the colorful bulbs gave the entire display the appearance of a starburst having fallen from the sky.

He checked the dashboard clock—9:15 p.m.

Time to find out where the hell I am.

He donned his gloves, hopped from the truck, and trudged through calf-deep snow toward the dwelling. He noted the crooked column of smoke rising from the chimney. Someone was in there keeping warm, he fancied. He climbed the porch steps stacked with freshly fallen flakes. Two twelve-paned windows, through which he glimpsed the soft glimmer of candlelight, flanked the front entrance. A child's sleigh and shovel were propped against one of the porch railings. A pinecone wreath decked the door.

He knocked. Moments later the door swung open. There to greet him was a young girl of seven or eight wearing a red and black plaid dress and a bright smile on her face. Her light brown tresses were knotted to the back with a red ribbon. "Hi," she said with child-like verve.

"Hi. Are your parents home?" Adam asked.

"No, my mother is away. She'll be back in a few minutes."

"And your father?"

"He no longer lives here," she said, the smile fading from her face.

"Well, why don't I wait in my truck till she comes back," Adam said, nodding to his pickup.

"Are you lost?" she asked.

"Yes. Is it that easy to tell?"

"People are always getting lost on this road," she said and took a step back. "Why don't you come on in? Brush the snow off yourself first, though."

"I really shouldn't. Didn't your mother warn you about talking to strangers?"

"Yes, but I'm a good judge of men," she said through a confident smile.

"Does your mother know that?" he asked.

"Yes. She's the one who taught me all about them," she said and repeated her invitation for him to enter.

Against his better judgment and that of all mankind, Adam followed her into the cabin, brushing the snow from his jacket and removing his gloves before entering.

"You can sit there," she said, pointing to an armchair while skipping across the room to hop onto a small couch.

The soft light of the cabin's interior was in sharp contrast to the glitter of the exterior. Flameless candles encased in mason jars-lined windowsills and a rock mantel that crowned a stone fireplace within whose pit rose lambent flames from logs reduced to embers. Tucked in a corner of the living room was a small, but sturdy pine tree adorned with tiers of blue twinkle lights and topped by an angel. A large Indian rug lay centered on the room's dark hardwood floor. Mixing with the scent of pine was the aroma of cinnamon sticks hanging from the railings of a narrow wooden staircase leading to what Adam presumed was a lofted bedroom.

"What's your name?" she asked, folding her legs beneath her.

"Adam. And yours?" he asked, setting aside his unease for the moment.

"Noelle, with two *e's* and two *l's*," she said. "I was born two days before Christmas."

"Your birthday was yesterday?"

"Yes. My mother gave me this dress I'm wearing."

5

"Nice. And now you'll be getting more presents."

"Yes, yes!" she said, bouncing from the couch to the tree where she began snatching presents one by one from beneath it, checking the gift tags on each. "This one is for me," she announced, whereupon she grabbed another. "This one is also for me," she said and selected another. "This one is for Shirley Mitchell, a friend of my mom's." She picked up another. "This is for Preston Marshall. I don't know who he is." And on she went, sorting through the pile until she reached the final one, holding it out for him to see. "And this one is for you," she said.

Adam tilted his head. "You sure that has my name on it?"

"It doesn't have any name on it. My mom says you should always keep a spare present in case someone shows up that you weren't expecting."

"You know, Noelle. I think you should save it for someone you know, maybe a friend or member of the family who might show up unexpectedly."

She placed the present back under the tree and at once skipped back to the couch, her hair flapping back and forth to her every step. "Are you married?" she asked.

"No."

"Why not?"

"Nobody will have me."

She threw a hand to her mouth and giggled.

"You needn't laugh so hard," Adam said, feigning a bruised ego.

"You're probably trying too hard," she said.

"And you're probably right,"

"Where are you from?" she asked.

"Florida."

"Really? Have you seen an alligator?"

"Yes."

"Did he try and bite you?"

"No."

"Why not?"

"Because I'm good at running in circles. Gators like to run in straight lines."

"Like this?" she asked, jumping to her feet and skipping sideways to

6

the left and right in a semi-circle, as if practicing a square dance step.

"You got it," Adam said in appreciation. "You'll never get eaten by a gator."

Noelle returned to the couch, obviously pleased with her performance.

"Say, do you know how I can get on the interstate from this road?" Adam asked, dimming the light-heartedness.

"Sure. We do it nearly every day. You go back down the road until you come to this other road right before the interstate. You take a right on it and after about a mile, you'll run into another road that lets you onto the highway. Are you leaving?"

"I was hoping your mother would be back by now."

"I thought she would be. She's usually not this late," she said, ostensibly unconcerned. "I know what! You could be my babysitter till she gets back, if you like."

What choice did he have and what kind of mother did she have were the two questions occupying his mind at the moment.

"I know what we can do while we're waiting," Noelle said, again bouncing from the couch. "We can make snow cream."

"That's a new one on me," Adam said inattentively, unable to tame his growing unease.

Noelle leaped to her feet and bounded to a small galley kitchen then returned with an oaken bucket in hand. "You take this outside and fill it with fresh snow. Make sure it's clean and soft snow...no yellow stuff."

Adam followed orders, lugged the bucket outside and swiped it into a fresh snow bank, filling it to the brim.

"Good," Noelle said, inspecting his haul. "We have to make it fast before it melts."

Adam leaned against the kitchen wall and watched her go to work, scooping up handfuls of the flakes and placing them in a large bowl, before stirring in some cream, sugar, and vanilla. "Sometimes we will mix in an egg, but not tonight," she said.

She stirred the mixture until it was the right texture, grabbed two serving bowls, filled them with the mixture, dropped in spoons, and handed one of the bowls to Adam who gamely downed a sample. "Tastes like homemade ice cream," he said.

They retired to the living room to enjoy the snack. "The only problem eating this is it makes you sleepy," Noelle said between bites.

"Do you know where your mother went?" Adam asked. "I saw a car parked in the carport. Is that her car?"

"Yes," she answered, finishing off the snow cream.

"How did she get where she was going?"

"She was just going for a walk. She likes walking alone in the woods when it's snowing. She usually doesn't go far."

"Shall we do the dishes?" Adam suggested.

"I'll do them," Noelle said, snatching her empty bowl from a coffee table and stepping across the room to grab Adam's dish.

"You sure you don't need some help?" he asked.

"I can do them," she responded and headed off to the kitchen.

Several loud snaps from remaining embers drew Adam's attention to the fireplace. "The fire's about ready to go out," he called to her. "Do you have any more logs?"

"There are some in the woodshed out back. I'll get more as soon as I finish the dishes."

"I'll get them," he said.

Adam donned his gloves and exited the cabin through the front entrance, circling it to the back. The snowstorm gave no indication of abating, piling drifts around trunks of trees and atop the cabin and carport. As he trudged further along, he found himself gradually moving out from beneath the aurora of lights and into the darkness. It was like stepping out from a colored film into a black and white one. Surrounding trees no longer bore decorative ornaments but stood draped in sheets of white. Pieces of their dark bark protruded through the sheets like bodily features, giving them the appearance of hooded Klansmen monitoring his every move.

The woodshed was sizable, maybe twelve by twenty feet with a slanted roof. Approaching it, Adam noted the shed's door was slightly ajar. He checked for footprints and found the heavy snowfall had covered up trail markings for the most part. On second glance, however, faint outlines remained despite the growing accumulation.

Adam nudged the door open with his arm into a shed-full of dark shadows. He stepped inside and paused, letting his eyes adjust to what little light was able to seep in through the opened doorway. Along the far side of the shed, he could make out a large white tarp spread over a mound of something. A pile of logs, he presumed. He edged in its direction but he had barely taken two steps when he bumped his shoulder against an object seemingly suspended in mid-air from the give of it. Startled, he took a step back to focus on the obstruction. Incredulous to what he was seeing, he hurried to the door and shoved it further open to allow in whatever additional light was available. A second look confirmed the worst. A rope was attached to a wooden beam running across the top of the shed. At the end of the rope was a noose, its loop stretched tightly around the neck of a woman's body. A stepladder lay on the floor beneath her.

Noelle's mother was no longer missing.

Adam removed a glove and checked for a pulse on the chance she might still be alive. As expected, her life had been choked out of her. He donned his glove again and wiped the portion of her wrist he had pressed with his fingers. While so doing, a gust of wind entered through the open doorway, followed quickly by the creak of wood as the beam above labored against the weight of the cadaver below. Circling the corpse, Adam carefully eyed the floor beneath it lest he contaminate evidence. For want of light, his observations were superficial at best. He conducted a quick visual exam of the body, noting the clothing, arms, hands, and fingers. Fearful Noelle might decide to join him at any moment, he stepped briskly to the doorway to sneak a peek at the cabin. She was nowhere around. Stepping back inside, he moved to the pile of firewood, lifted the canvas and grabbed four of the logs. He took one last look around before heading back, the wood weighing heavy under his arm, but nothing compared to what was weighing on his mind.

"You're just in time. The fire's about ready to go out," Noelle said on his return.

She had settled into a fetal position on the couch. A blanket she had retrieved while he was gone covered her from the waist down. A throw pillow served as her headrest. "We were supposed to go to midnight Mass tonight but couldn't because of the snow," she said, stifling a yawn. "I hope mother gets home soon or she'll have a tough time waking up in the morning."

Adam pulled back the copper screen protector from the fireplace, placed two logs on the pulsating embers, set aside the two others, readjusted the screen, and returned to the armchair.

"Do you ever go to midnight Mass?" she asked, stretching her legs while trying to muzzle another yawn.

"Not as often as I should," he answered, thinking a good prayer or two might be in order right about now.

"Did your mother receive any phone calls earlier tonight?" he asked.

"She got one. Why?"

"It might explain why she was late. Do you know who it was from?"

"No," she said, tossing her body back and forth, trying to find a comfortable position.

"Well, since she's running late, why don't you go ahead and get some sleep?"

"Are you going to babysit me?" she asked.

"Yes. I'll babysit you."

"Then tell me a bedtime story."

"A bedtime story?"

"Yes. My babysitters always tell me a bedtime story or else I don't go to sleep."

Adam sighed a deep breath. "What kind of a story would you like to hear?"

"One with magic in it."

Adam wished he could make what he had just seen disappear. He pondered his options while scooting the armchair next to the couch. "Okay, here we go. A long time ago there was this old man who lived on a small island in the middle of the sea with his beautiful daughter…"

"How did they get there?" she asked.

"The old man's evil brother with the help of an evil king forced them into a tiny boat and they drifted around until they landed there."

"There was no one else on the island?"

"No, it was deserted," Adam said. "Anyway, they lived in a cave made out of rocks…"

"Why did they live in a cave?"

"Because there was nothing else to live in," he said, anxious to hurry the story along. "It was in this cave the old man stored all of his books, which were his second most important possession."

"What was his most important?"

"His daughter, of course. The books were important since they were all about magic, his favorite subject. Magic became very useful for him because a witch had lived on the island before they arrived, as did many good spirits."

"Spirits are like angels?"

"Yes. They are very much alike and because the good spirits refused to carry out the witch's wicked commands, she imprisoned them in the trunks of trees before she died. By using the magic he'd learned from his books, the old man was able to release the spirits who thereafter became his servants. With these spirits he had the power to control the winds and waves of the sea."

"Why did he want to control the winds and the waves?" she asked.

"Because he wanted to create a big storm. His evil brother and the evil king who helped him were aboard a ship passing by the island. The king's son was also aboard the ship."

"He wanted to hurt them?"

"No, he didn't. What he wanted was to bring his brother and the king to justice for what they had done to him and his daughter. However, when they ended up in the presence of the old man, they were very remorseful, saying how sorry they were for what they had done."

"Did he believe they were sorry?"

"Yes, and because he believed them, he gave them his forgiveness. He also saw to it that their ship was left safe in the harbor."

"He and his daughter were left alone again?"

"No, he and his daughter accompanied them back home. As a matter of fact, the old man's daughter and the king's son fell in love and became engaged to be married."

"What happened to the spirits?"

"Before he left the old man set them free."

"Why?"

"To help other people who become stranded and left all alone. One of those good spirits is always ready to help someone when they feel deserted."

"Like a guardian angel?"

"Like a guardian angel."

Noelle wiggled her body back into a fetal position. "I think I'll sleep right here on the couch. I like lying next to the tree," she said, turning her gaze on him. "If I'm not awake when you leave, are you going to come back and see me?"

"Yes. I'll come back to see you."

"Promise?"

"I promise."

The balm of snow cream and flickering firelight sent Noelle adrift on a deep sleep. Confident her slumber was sound, Adam rose from his chair and walked to a small desk tucked behind the staircase. A phone, along with pieces of stationary and a few unopened letters were scattered on its surface. He picked up the phone with his gloved hand and dialed 9-1-1.

"This is 9-1-1. What is your emergency?" a woman asked in the customary mechanical tone.

"I'm calling to report a woman's death by hanging—"

"Sir, where are you calling from?"

Adam glanced at one of the envelopes on the desk. "Five-two-five Creekside Heights," he said, knowing the address was already on the woman's computer screen.

"Where did this hanging occur?" she asked.

"It occurred in a woodshed behind the woman's home. There is a child of hers asleep in the home. She is not aware of the hanging. I strongly recommend the responders bring along a child counselor."

"Is this a suicide?" she asked.

"Maybe...maybe not," he answered and hung up the phone, avoiding the "please stay on the line" he knew was coming.

Adam shifted the armchair back to its proper position and took one last look around the interior of the cabin, wiping clean any place where he may have left prints, before moving to Noelle's side. He reached down and drew the blanket above her shoulders. "I'll be back," he whispered under his breath.

Quietly exiting the cabin, Adam decided to take an inspection tour around the perimeter of it via the woods. Weaving in and out of the shadowy trees, he relied on the ghostly light from the cabin's adornments

12

that appeared to be following him along the way to spot anything out of the ordinary. Satisfied no one was lurking within the vicinity, he trudged back to his truck and turned the ignition, waking the engine. Flipping on the wipers to brush aside the intervening accumulation of snow, he surveyed the surrounding landscape, noting intermittent stands of spruce trees lining a small incline to the left of the roadway. He wheeled the pickup across the road and up the hillside. Despite some fishtailing, he was able to climb it in a semi-circular path, eventually maneuvering the vehicle behind a clump of trees, their branches offering sufficient separation to allow him a clear view of the cabin. Satisfied with his perch, he shut off the engine and began his wait.

For well over an hour Adam kept his gaze fastened on the cabin. Snowflakes the size of cotton balls drifted downward, forming a beaded curtain through which he kept watch. Occasionally, he would run the engine to warm the cab. To his surprise, a couple of vehicles in the interim had slogged their way down the roadway. By now, the snowfall had turned to snow showers, starting and stopping with clockwork regularity. During one of the longer intermissions, he hopped from the pickup and leaned his head back to gaze at length at the clear canvas of the Colorado night sky. Flickering stars hung in the heavens like added ornaments strung to the earthly ones originating not a snowball's throw from where he stood.

It was another light show, a sweep of headlights backed by flashers that drew Adam's attention back to the roadway. Two emergency vehicles, their sirens silent, had arrived with the first responders. He quickly re-entered the cab and checked the dashboard clock—five minutes past midnight. The sight of the cabin slowed the crews' advance, the muffled whirr of their vehicles coming to a stop directly below Adam's vantage point. A man and woman exited each vehicle. One pair headed for the front door, the other pair, flashlights in hand, clomped their way toward the woodshed to the rear of the home. The woman arriving at the front door knocked immediately and waited...knocked again and waited.

"Give her time," Adam whispered from afar.

She knocked once again. This time the door swung open. For a minute, the woman engaged Noelle in conversation, at the end of which the child stepped back to allow the two to enter.

Adam ignited the pickup's engine the moment the cabin door closed. He edged the truck further along its semi-circular path back to the roadway. By the time he was out from under the glow of lights, the snow showers resumed, once again bringing a quiet to the landscape, if not his mind.

CHAPTER TWO

"The answer is simple, Reggie. I wanted to be on the outside looking in for this one. Call it a control thing, if you like."

"What makes you think it wasn't a suicide?"

"The girl."

"Surely you know there have been times when a parent has taken his or her life in the proximity of a child."

"Not this child," Adam said. "She's special. No mother would do that to her."

"Sounds like someone was smitten. Isn't every child special to their mother?"

"Yeah, you're right," Adam said.

"Why didn't you give me a call?" Reggie asked.

"From the cabin? Adam asked back. "If I had, it wouldn't have been long before they showed up at your doorstep. They do check phone records, you know."

Adam sat with his former colleague at a kitchen table in a condo tucked in the foothills a few miles southwest of Colorado Springs. Christmas morning had brought clear skies and sunshine but not a lot of holiday mirth to the Reginald Fielding abode. The two gazed absentmindedly out a bay window overlooking a multi-sloped landscape blanketed by the overnight snow. Each held a mug of warm mulled wine in hand.

Adam took a sip of the drink before continuing with his account. "It was dark and I wasn't able to examine the body closely. Plus, I was worried about the girl. I needed to get her help."

"So the mother was already dead by the time you arrived?"

"Yes. If I had to guess, dead less than an hour, maybe even minutes."

"Ambushed?"

"Yes, though again it's speculation. I only had time for a cursory examination."

"Nobody hiding in the bushes or corners of the house?"

"No, not as far as I could determine."

Reggie fingered his mug. "Any inkling as to a motive?" he asked.

"None whatsoever. From what I could tell, there were no signs of sexual assault and robbery seems unlikely."

"Personal then?"

"Yes. It had personal stamped all over it."

"So you start with the family members…right?"

Adam nodded his agreement. "It was no stranger in the night. I'd bet on it."

Reggie shoved his chair away from the table with a wake-me-up grating sound and walked to the sink to rinse out his empty cup. Everything about the guy was big, Adam observed—big head—big chest—big arms—big feet—and a big boisterous laugh he'd spring on occasion. The sole feature not big was his hair. He had none, though he did sport a mountaineer beard perhaps to make up for it.

"How convenient for the killer," Reggie said, reclaiming his chair. "You come along at a critical moment and now the authorities will be chasing your tail."

"They have very little to go by, except for what the girl can tell them."

"Which is?"

"My name is Adam. I'm from Florida. I drive a red truck." Adam rose from his chair to empty his mug in the sink. "Listen, Reggie. I don't want to put you in any jeopardy," he said. "I can go hole up in a motel room."

"Hole up and do what? How are you going to get around without being spotted? We agreed you'd spend a week here. Just back your truck into my carport so no one will spot the Florida plates and let me do the driving. While they're looking for you, we'll be looking for the killer. Of course all those fun activities I had in store are now out the window, but that's a good thing."

"How so?"

"We can go back to being the security team we once were in the Air Force."

"You mean spending our time reporting burned out lights, checking identification cards, conducting crowd control at air shows, and performing guard duty at all hours of the day…those sorts of things," Adam said. "Not exactly officer duty stuff."

"Speaking of officer duty, did I ever tell you I was an Air Force Academy reject?" Reggie asked between sips of wine.

"Before or after you entered?" Adam asked, somewhat surprised at the announcement.

"Before," Reggie replied. "I received a nomination to attend from a local congressman. He was all into athletics and felt I could bolster their football program."

"You were making a name for yourself in high school football?"

"Defensive end—first team all-state, I'll have you know. I was the local boy who was on a fast lane to playing for the Falcons. That was until I got derailed."

"What happened?"

"My academics didn't measure up to my quarterback sacks. I was deficient in math and science skills, they informed me. I'll be honest. I still don't know trigonometry from Deuteronomy. I blamed it on the school I was attending. They blamed it on me. On top of that, I was in a very competitive district. Only so many are allowed into the academy based on how well rounded they are in just about every aspect of life."

"So, you ended up entering the Air Force the old fashioned way, like me," Adam said.

"Yeah, I don't know whether I was cut out to be an officer and a gentleman anyway. Certainly, not a gentleman," Reggie added with a grin.

"You did okay for yourself," Adam said, tossing him an encouraging word.

"*Okay* is correct," Reggie replied. "I should have done what you did and took advantage of the G. I. Bill and continued my education."

"Sure, look what it's done for me. Prepared me for a life on the run."

"I wouldn't call it a life on the run, more a short detour," Reggie pointed out. "What was it again you majored in?"

"English."

"Never understood that major. You spend four years learning about a language you already know?"

Adam smiled. "You read all these other people's views of the world and from them you form your own."

"And that prepares you for all the twists and turns of life?"

"Not as well as trigonometry does, I've learned," Adam said.

"Well, back to the point I was making about us going back to being a security team," Reggie said. "Didn't we always hanker to step up the crime ladder a rung or two...tackle a more challenging case if we could? Well, here's our opportunity. Beats breaking a leg on the ski slopes. Sure as hell tops back and forth banter with bar flies."

"How's the bartending life working out for you?"

"It isn't. When you're not serving drinks or food, people sit and stare at you as if they expect you to perform for them."

"Perform what?" Adam asked.

"Damned if I know. Song and dance of some kind, I suppose. One time I came out from behind the bar and some guy commented he wasn't aware I had legs, having only seen me from the waist up for all the time he spent there."

"That's the worst thing to happen to you?"

"No. The worst was the night we had a packed house and a woman eating at the bar suddenly stood up in the middle of her meal and barfed all over the counter. The splatter sent other customers scrambling from their stools. The perpetrator sauntered off to the restroom while the staff rushed over to clean the mess up. You'd think the embarrassment of it all would have kept her from showing her face again, but no, she trots right back to reclaim her seat and reorder another dinner, which reminds me— I put in Christmas dinner reservations for us at a nice Italian restaurant down the road."

"You mean you're not going to cook up a little something for us?" Adam quipped.

"Not unless you want a hot dog for your holiday meal."

Adam rose from his chair and strolled to the bay window to fix his gaze on the glistening landscape. "I wonder how Noelle is spending the day," he pondered in the midst of his reverie.

"Don't worry. I'm sure she's being taken care of," Reggie responded.

Adam returned to the table, deciding it was time to shake off his blue funk, if he was to get started on solving his predicament. "Okay, where do we begin?"

"Like we agreed, you start with the family members," Reggie said. "Did the little girl mention any?"

"Other than her mother, she made mention of a father who no longer lived with them, which I take to mean she was either divorced or separated. She never mentioned any siblings. I'm fairly certain she's an only child from the way she talked and the appearance of the house."

"Did you get any names?"

"The mother's name is Rita Feldman. It was printed on some stationary scattered across a desk."

"Shouldn't be difficult to get the ex-hubby's name. Anything else of note?"

"Couple of odds and ends. Noelle said her mother received a phone call earlier in the evening. There could be a connection. Someone could have called and asked her to meet them outside to settle whatever it was that was boiling between them."

"Pure conjecture," Reggie countered. "Anything else?"

"Yes. As I was approaching the cabin in my pickup, I nearly collided with a car coming in the opposite direction."

"I'd ask whose fault it was but you're asking the question of who might it have been?"

"Nobody's fault considering the conditions. We met at the top of a hill. Neither of us saw the other until the last second when we swerved to avoid each other. As to who, how would I know?"

"What model of car?" Reggie asked.

"Land Rover...late model."

"What do you make of it?"

"It had to be something important for him to risk driving in those conditions," Adam said.

"Did he have a white beard and fat belly?"

"Could well have had both, as little as I saw of him."

Adam scooted his chair from the table and again walked to the bay window, stepping into a beam of sunlight that shed a soft light across the caramel carpeted living room floor. "You know, I can't help but think it was providence that brought me to that cabin," he said.

"The Rockies are known for spitting out surprise storms," Reggie advised, dousing the notion. "Tomorrow morning's paper may have a story on the incident, though I've heard nothing on the news thus far."

"The cops will hold off announcing it until there's a determination of whether or not it was a suicide."

"And if it is?" Reggie asked.

"Then the air goes out of our balloon."

"And you remain a wanted man, maybe not on the level of a Billy the Kid but, still, a wanted man."

* * * *

Though the coverage was modest, the incident made the morning paper, the headline coming below the fold on page two of the local section.

Sheriff's Officials Investigating Suspicious Death

The body of a thirty-eight-year-old woman was found hanging in a woodshed at the rear of a home located on Creekside Heights Road in western El Paso County. An anonymous caller summoned emergency personnel to the home Christmas Eve. Upon arrival, they discovered the deceased woman later identified as Rita Feldman. Detectives are asking anyone who may have information regarding the incident to contact the Sheriff's Department. Investigators are also seeking the identity of an unknown male driving a late model red pickup with Florida license tags who was seen in the vicinity at the time of the incident.

"Did Noelle make a point of checking your license plates?" Reggie asked setting aside the paper.

Adam smiled. "No, they're speculating based on what she told them. Otherwise, what good would it do them to state *a late model red pickup*? Everyone in these parts must know of someone who drives one of those…right?"

"Anything else to draw from it?" Reggie asked.

"The article?"

"Yes."

Adam glanced at the opened paper on the table. "They're not buying the suicide argument, either. My guess is they're waiting on the medical examiner's report to verify their suspicions."

"'Unknown male seen in the vicinity.' You were in the home for God's sake. Surely, they know that from talking to Noelle."

"And you should know they're holding back pieces of the puzzle only the perpetrator would be aware of, like there was a child in the house."

Reggie slapped his thighs and sprung from his chair. "Okay, why don't I get on my computer and see what I can come up with regarding Rita Feldman," he said. "It'll give us a start."

"While you're busy with that, would you mind if I took a break and went for a walk? I could use a little down time right about now before jumping into the fray."

"Not at all. Have at it. Breathing mountain air can do wonders for a guy's mental state. There's a walking trail directly behind the complex. It'll lead you further up into the hills. A creek runs alongside it."

Adam bundled up and headed out onto the trail. A foggy mist hovered over the landscape, dulling the sheen of its fresh white carpet. More in keeping with his mood, he mused. Thin shards of ice covered the bordering creek. From below them arose the soothing gurgles of the stream, easing his troubled mind. Contributing to his newfound contentment was the absence of insects and people, always a plus when in search of a natural high.

Midway through his hike, a lone crow perched on an overhanging tree limb cackled its presence, lifting Adam out of his mindless state. Reaching the summit of a small hill, he paused to take in a deep lungful of the crisp morning air. From where he stood, he was witness to the full breadth and beauty of the mountains rising in the distance. He lingered a while longer before taking one final panoramic view of the peaks appearing ghostlike in the mist. Turning to head back down the slope, his thoughts drew to the issue awaiting him. Nagging him was the question of exactly how foolish he was to leave the scene of a possible homicide. Foolish enough to launch him into another round of second guessing, he quickly realized. Why not turn yourself in, tell them what you know, and sit on the sidelines to watch events unfold? It seemed the sensible thing to do, but for Adam there were deeper motivations for sticking to the course he had chosen. For one thing, he was already in the game. What competitor wants to take himself out of a contest before it's decided? For another, there was the personal element. The same sense of fear and helplessness he knew Noelle was experiencing he also lived through at an early age. He too was a young child at the time, living the happy kid's life when tragedy struck. The first inkling of it came on a school playground. He was summoned from recess and taken to the principal's office. Next thing he knew he was sitting in a chair surrounded by serious-looking people who were informing him his parents had been killed in a tragic auto accident. From that moment on, his world became a tempest of emotions tossing him every which way but home, for he no longer had one. An only child, bereft of close relatives, he eventually ended up in the care of foster parents whose goal was to adopt. Strangely enough, it was a succession of bad colds and cavities, including an abscessed tooth that laid the foundation for a successful bonding. Lots of touching and comforting by Mr. and Mrs. Fraley not only salved his physical discomfort, it banished his initial reluctance to the relationship. Looking back, he could say with certainty that any and all accomplishments he had achieved in life could be directly attributed to his parents…both sets.

Adam reached the bottom of the hill, his lungs cleansed, his second-guessing over, and his mind back on the game.

* * * *

"Anything of note?" Adam asked, fresh from taking a hot shower following his hike.

"Yes, one item in particular," Reggie said, keeping his gaze focused on a computer nearly the size of the desktop. "Pull up a chair."

Adam grabbed one from the kitchen, slid it aside the desk, and took a seat.

Reggie turned his attention to a stack of printouts he had made, picking through the pile in earnest. "First of all, Rita and Arlen Feldman were divorced eight months ago. Nothing unusual about the settlement, citing irreconcilable differences as the cause of the breakup. What I did find of interest separate from the divorce was that Arlen Feldman was the subject of a civil lawsuit filed by a group of investors a year and a half ago."

"He was a stockbroker?"

"Called himself a financial planner."

"How large a suit?" Adam asked.

"Big enough to make the paper. The plaintiffs claimed he diverted and misappropriated nearly a million bucks of their money."

"How'd he manage to do that?"

Reggie leaned back in his chair and eyed the computer screen from a distance. "He set up this so-called settlement services firm that specialized in investing money for personal injury victims who were awarded lump sum lawsuit settlements. His clients were mainly widows and orphans of individuals killed in auto accidents. The widows, especially, became financially dependent on his services."

"Now there's a targeted audience if I ever heard of one," Adam said. "How'd he work it?"

"His stated aim was to set up trusts utilizing the settlement funds and invest the money in high grade government securities to provide a regular monthly income for the victims. Instead, he ran a typical Ponzi scheme, paying off early investors with later victims' money, all the while raking off funds for personal gain. From early on he was making a series of unauthorized transactions in high risk investments."

"There was no oversight of his operation?" Adam asked.

"As a small independent operator, he was not subject to an internal compliance office. He was his own monitor."

"So he intended it as a scam from the start," Adam said.

"Whether he planned it as one or it simply ballooned into one is probably a question only Feldman could answer. To the victims it is a moot point."

"Ironic, isn't it?" Adam observed. "Takes know-how to concoct a scheme like that, not to mention the talent to implement it."

"From what I gather, Feldman has the credentials to cook one up. Along with a financial license, he has a law degree," Reggie pointed out. "Think of the referrals he could have generated through his contacts in the legal community. He easily could have set himself up as the go-to guy for the suddenly rich."

"What went wrong?" Adam asked.

"What usually goes wrong in those sorts of schemes—the promised returns fail to materialize. Questions you may have go unanswered. Quarterly statements do not show up in the mail, or appear vague, or differ from what you were led to believe, and so on."

"You speak like a knowledgeable insider on this, Reggie."

His host cast him a deadpanned look. "If you recall, Adam, I do have an associate degree in finance. I've done my share of investing. As a matter of fact, while you were on your little hike, I called a stockbroker buddy of mine to see if he could shed some light on the lawsuit. It turns out, he knew Feldman in a professional capacity. He said the guy worked hard to come across as smooth and accomplished, going out of his way to join civic organizations and participate in community events. He also worked out of a lush office, which gave him the appearance of a reputable businessman. Put simply, he looked the part."

"I take it Feldman beat the rap?"

"He sure did. Acquitted on all charges."

"How did he manage that?"

"According to my source, there was no money trail to prove he was diverting or misappropriating funds to his personal benefit. Furthermore, there was no evidence he was making lush purchases or going on spending sprees. The bottom line was the plaintiffs were unable to prove he was raking off their money. He may have been making bad investments, but making bad investments is not enough to convict a guy."

"If a civil suit failed, there's no way a criminal case could be made," Adam said.

"Which is why the DA's office never attempted to make one," Reggie said. "Feldman was like a guy standing on a street corner with his pockets turned inside out, shouting to everyone who would listen 'look, I've got nothing.'"

"There were no bank records to indicate he was making unusual deposits or withdrawals?" Adam asked.

"Apparently, several of his elderly, wealthier clients went so far as to turn over to him under-the-mattress stacks of cash to make their investments. They trusted him more than the brick and mortar banks. Needless to say, the investments were never made. To answer your question, there were no out of the ordinary deposits or withdrawals."

"The question then becomes what did he do with the money?" Adam asked. "Did he have a secretary or an office manager handling transaction records?"

"Yes, a woman by the name of Daniela Diaz, now known as Daniela Feldman."

"He married her?"

"Yes, not long after the divorce."

"What are the chances she knows where all the goodies are hidden?" Adam asked.

"I'd say they're pretty good. Who knows? It could have been what sparked her into doing the proposing—you know, marry me or else."

"And Rita Feldman, what's her role in all of this, and did it get her killed?"

"No doubt Arlen Feldman's at the top of the suspect list," Reggie said. "You know how it goes in these kinds of cases; the husband is guilty until proven innocent."

"Did he have the motive and does he have the alibi are two questions I'm sure investigators already have addressed," Adam said, drumming his fingers on the desk. Now that their enterprise has folded, any idea how they are making a living without having to dip into the haul they've stashed away?"

"One of the other bits of info my source passed on was that Daniela is currently working as a manager at La Gulch Cantina, an upscale Mexican restaurant not far from here."

"What is keeping them from picking up and leaving?" Adam asked. "Is she originally from this area?"

"Mexico. Santa Cruz to be specific."

"All the more reason to pick up and leave. Skipping the country wouldn't be a bad option for them right about now."

"Chances are they're waiting for things to play out regarding the investigation into his ex-wife's death. Skipping out might not be the wisest move at the moment, unless he has an ironclad alibi."

"You say La Gulch Cantina is not far from here. I'm thinking maybe I'd like to have lunch there today," Adam said.

"To speak with her?" Reggie asked

"At least to look her in the eye," Adam replied. "Are you up for lunch?"

"I've got a job interview at a large construction outfit later this morning. It shows promise. I need to restart my professional career before I let the bar business get into my blood, if it already hasn't."

"Safety work?"

"Yes. Why don't I drop you off at the restaurant and pick you up later. It's a follow-up interview I have scheduled so it shouldn't take long."

"Sounds good," Adam said, standing to stretch his limbs.

"Oh, there's one other bit of info my source passed along to me," Reggie said, shutting down the computer.

"What's that?"

"Arlen Feldman drives a late model Land Rover."

CHAPTER THREE

Vernon Jolly was a husky man with sloped forehead, retreating hairline, ruddy complexion, and large hazel eyes that had "intelligent" stamped on each of them. A few of his colleagues in the sheriff's department had taken to calling him Mr. Tomato for his propensity to wear bulky clothes of varying shades of red. Others felt the color scheme, along with his surname and the slight stoop to his gait, as if he was lugging a gift bag over his shoulder, was particularly apt during the holiday season. The more astute, however, viewed it as the attire of a hunter, a designation most agreed best fit his reputation as a skilled homicide detective.

How others viewed him was of least concern to Jolly. At the moment, he was more concerned with departmental procedure, particularly as it related to the Arlen Feldman case. While he liked to think of himself as practical and thorough, he would be the first to acknowledge he was not always diplomatic in his dealings with co-workers, as his supervisors had been pointing out to him in his personnel evaluations for the past eighteen years. So what if others considered him aloof? As he told his supervisor, he was no good at small talk. Not that he had anything against it, mind you. He simply wasn't skilled at it. If you wanted someone to talk about the finer points of a new pair of shoes for hours on end, he was not your man. On the other hand, if you wished to discuss the footprints left at a crime scene, he was your guy. It also was no secret he preferred working alone, viewing his profession as a craft in which there was but one craftsman assigned whose job was to build a case clue by clue with his imprint on it. Which was why he was none too thrilled to have a partner assigned to him in the Feldman investigation. The reason for it, his boss patiently explained, was simple. The folks from administration felt a specialist from the Children's Victims Unit should come on board, given there was a child at the center of the case. Never mind the fact he had two daughters of his own who were once Noelle Feldman's age. Should that not count for something? Not that it mattered in the long run. Let them mix and match according to the fashions of the day. The end result would be the same. He would catch a killer, alone or not, and in a manner that ensured justice for the victims.

Ending Jolly's ruminations was the woman who was the subject of them. He spotted Carlita Perez through the department's interview room window heading his way with a large notebook clutched against her chest. He had bumped into her on occasion while conducting other business but never to the extent of forming a professional opinion of her work. To Jolly, she was the stately woman who wore long dresses when not in uniform and spoke with a soft voice, enunciating her words carefully so as not to confuse listeners with their meaning.

"I read the medical examiner's report," she said, joining him at the interview room table. "He seems definite about it being a homicide."

"It was an amateurish effort to make it look like a suicide," Jolly said in his gruff voice.

"There were no signs of a struggle," Carlita pointed out.

"More than likely he attacked her when she had her back turned to him," Jolly said. "A hanging always leaves an inverted V bruise and can easily be distinguished from a straight line ligature marking, which is what the victim had. As the report indicated, her bruises and abrasions were deep around the neck, suggesting the murderer used excessive force. Besides, hanging is not the normal method of choice for women looking to commit suicide. They prefer the sleeping pill way out."

"A passion killing then?" Carlita asked.

"Yes and by a male most likely."

"He brought the rope with him?"

"Yes, along with whatever he used as the ligature. The medical examiner said it looked as if he cut off an end piece of the rope and used it as the weapon."

"The ligature piece is missing?" she asked.

"Yes, he took it with him; apparently, though I'm sure he's dumped it by now."

At that moment, a desk sergeant stuck his head through the door. "They're here," he said.

"Show them in," Jolly replied.

"Did she attend her mother's burial service I wonder?" Carlita whispered.

"I don't believe so," Jolly said. "Her mother's church handled the service. She was cremated according to her wishes."

Carlita opened her notebook. "I jotted down a few questions I'd like to ask her," she said, as if asking for permission.

"Go right ahead," he said. "I understand this is your area of expertise, so I'll let you take the lead."

The desk sergeant returned, accompanied by a rotund, moon-faced woman dressed in a gray suit from Children's Protective Services. At her side was Noelle Feldman, bundled in a green jacket reaching to her knees.

Carlita turned her soft gaze on the child. "How are you feeling, Noelle?" she asked.

"Okay, I guess," she answered, digging her hands deeper into the pockets of her jacket.

"Just okay?" Carlita asked.

Noelle removed her hands from her pockets and clasped them in her lap. "Yeah, it's kind of hard."

"I'm sure it is, honey," Carlita said. "From what everyone tells me, you're a strong little girl."

Jolly cleared his throat. "Do you think you could answer a few more questions for us, Noelle?" he asked, attempting Carlita's soft approach.

Noelle glanced at her escort who was busy maintaining a stoic face. "Yes," she said, returning her attention to the man sitting across from her.

"You told the officers on Christmas Eve a man you did not know showed up at your house unexpectedly. He told you he was lost so you invited him in to wait for your mother who was out taking a walk. You

29

said his name was Adam. You also said he was driving a red truck and that he was from Florida. Did we get all that right?"

Noelle shifted in her chair and nodded another yes.

"Is there anything else you can tell us about him? You said he was around thirty years old. What color hair did he have?"

"Brown," she answered immediately.

"Short? Long? Medium?"

"Medium."

"How big would you say he was—large, small, or medium?"

"Medium."

"And you said he was at your house for how long?"

Noelle shrugged her tiny shoulders. "I don't know."

"An hour or so maybe?"

"Yes, I guess. We talked for a while and made some snow cream," she said.

Jolly look to Carlita for an explanation.

"It's a winter treat, a mix of snow, cream, and sugar," she said.

"And vanilla," Noelle interjected.

"What else did you talk about?" Jolly asked.

"Mostly about alligators and Christmas. He also told me a bedtime story."

"What kind of a story?" Carlita asked.

"A magic story," she said.

"Noelle, honey, was he a nice man?" Carlita asked.

"Yes," she said, nodding vigorously.

"He didn't harm you in any way?"

"No. He was very nice."

"Noelle, did you ever hear your mother and father arguing?" Carlita asked.

The face of the Children's Protective Services woman went from stoic to stern on hearing the question. She turned to her young charge whose eyes welled with tears. "Are you okay?"

A brief silence settled over the room, before Noelle regained her composure. "Yes, I heard them argue once or twice," she said. "Oh, there is one more thing I remember."

"What's that?" Jolly interjected.

"Adam asked if my mother had received any phone calls before she went for her walk."

"Did she?" Jolly followed.

"She received one."

"You don't know who it was from or what it was about, do you?" he asked.

"No, she didn't say."

"And after a while you fell asleep and he was gone when the officers showed up at your door, right?" he asked.

"Yes."

"When you sleep, do you dream a lot, Noelle?" Carlita asked.

"Sometimes."

"Is there any chance you could have been dreaming all of this?"

"About Adam?"

"Yes."

She shook her head. "No. He was real."

"You have no idea where he was going after he left?" Jolly asked.

"No, but he did ask how he could get back to the interstate."

"Did he tell you before you went to sleep he was going to leave?" Carlita asked.

"No, but he did promise he would come back some day."

"Did he say for what, honey?"

"Yes, to see me."

* * * *

"Except for the phone call, not much new here, is there?" Carlita asked in their post-interview review. "Do you see any connection between the call and the homicide?"

"There's always the possibility of one," Jolly said, rubbing his chin. "About an hour ago we received the phone records. They show the call came from the Feldman home."

"Where he says he and his wife were spending Christmas Eve," Carlita said.

"Yes, it's his ironclad alibi and he's sticking to it. His wife also swears to it."

"Why call her on Christmas Eve?" Carlita asked. "Surely not to wish her a merry Christmas. To wish the child one? Maybe the ex-wife didn't want him speaking to her."

"Interesting this guy, Adam, asked her if there were any calls," Jolly said.

"Like he expected there to be one? Do you suppose it was Adam's job to distract the child while the killer was going about his business?"

"Right now everything is in the realm of possibility."

"If he wasn't the perpetrator, why would he leave?" Carlita asked.

"Good question."

"Something in his background that decides it for him, no doubt," she said. "Maybe a rap sheet?"

"Could be," Jolly said. "He made a point of not leaving any fingerprints."

"That little girl has experienced way too much pain for a seven-year-old," she said. "I can't imagine someone leaving her alone under those circumstances. And to think he told her a bedtime story. It doesn't mesh with him abandoning her."

"He didn't abandon her," Jolly replied matter-of-factly.

Carlita flashed him a perplexed look.

"There were tire tracks and footprints discovered behind a cluster of trees halfway up the incline from the cabin," Jolly explained. "He was babysitting from a distance. I'm guessing he left right after the response team arrived."

"Could anything else be determined from the tracks?" she asked.

"Nothing of substance. The tracks were faint though visible enough to conclude someone was there and not to take a leak."

"Maybe it was the killer and not this Adam guy."

"Killers don't hang around for no good reason, especially an altruistic one," Jolly countered.

Carlita checked through her notes. "There were a couple of domestic disturbance calls back when they were married. He was threatening violence but as usual with the wives, she refused to press charges. Says something about the volatile feelings between the two, however. Who knows? Adam could be the nice guy Noelle says he was."

"I'm not ready to jump to that conclusion at this point," Jolly said, adhering to the golden rule of detectives to keep an open mind and follow the evidence.

"What next?" Carlita asked.

Next was the reappearance of the desk sergeant, who strode through the open doorway bearing a message. "Got some news for you two," he said, waving a piece of paper in his hand.

"Let's hear it," Jolly said, settling back in his chair and clasping his hands in his lap.

The sergeant glanced down at the paper he held in hand. "We received a call from the Colorado Highway Patrol a while ago. They informed us a trucker called to let them know he was traveling Highway 24 Christmas Eve when he decided to pull off the road not far from Colorado Springs to wait out the storm. When he did, a pickup—a red pickup—that had been following him for some time also pulled off the road to park in front of him. For what reason the trucker wasn't sure. Could have been he was also going to call it a night. It all ended when the trucker flashed his high beams to let the guy know it was his space he was invading, causing the pickup driver to crank his engine back up and head back out onto the highway, but not before the trucker jotted down the guy's license plate number."

"The plate—out of state?" Jolly asked.

"Yep—Florida."

"Did you run them?"

"Yes. They belong to a guy by the name of Adam Fraley. He's from Tampa, Florida and a private investigator for an outfit called Adam Fraley Private Investigations."

"Any follow through?" Jolly asked, unable to mask his surprise at the revelation.

"We contacted the sheriff's department down there. They're going to send a couple of deputies over to his office to find out what they can. They'll get back to us shortly."

"Can you get a photo of him?" Carlita asked.

"We should be able to come up with one," he said.

"Thanks sergeant," Jolly said, as the trooper turned to leave.

Carlita closed her notebook. "Well, that makes matters more interesting, as if they weren't already," she said. "Do you suppose he was here working on a case? Who would hire a private investigator from

Florida and why?"

"It might explain his leaving the scene," Jolly said.

"In what way?"

"His professional instinct is to solve a crime, not leave it for someone else to unravel, particularly if he's working for a client."

"Which is exactly what he did for all intents and purposes—left it for someone else," she said.

"Not necessarily. Let's say everything he told the girl was true, that he was lost and accidentally stumbled upon the scene. His choice was to play witness or play investigator. He very well could have chosen the latter. He may be his own client."

"How can you be sure?"

"I'm not. At the moment, I'm living vicariously through him. After all, he may be way ahead of us in the investigation."

"He did leave the scene of a crime," Carlita pointed out. "He may also be way ahead of us in fleeing it."

"He reported it and left. Still, not a wise thing for him to do," Jolly responded.

"If freelancing the case is what he has in mind, somebody needs to remind him he does not work for the government. His job is not to arrest or prosecute, especially in this state where he may not even be licensed."

"When you boil it all down, Carlita, his job as a private investigator is to collect information and analyze it, the same as us."

"So, if a private investigator is tracking down a person or persons and then they become suspects in a crime, is he obligated to turn them over to the police?" she asked.

"From the private investigator's perspective, it depends if they are more useful to him in jail or not. They know how to toe the legal line."

"Meaning the priorities are dissimilar," she said with conviction. "Did you ever consider private eye work over this?"

"Most private eyes have a background in law enforcement. It's not a career you normally start from scratch," Jolly said. "You're right in saying they deal more with civil cases than criminal. The intricacies of the moral laws the justice system does not address are more their source of income—cheating spouses and the like, for instance."

"What's next on the agenda?"

"First off, we need to touch base with both Arlen and Daniela Feldman as soon as possible to alert them to this guy Fraley," he said. "If he is of a mind to take on the case, we could be following similar tracks, even crossing paths if we are lucky. Why don't you head over to La Gulch Cantina where Daniela works and brief her? Who knows? Fraley may have already contacted her. Meanwhile I'll track down her husband. See if he is aware of the mysterious interloper."

"Daniela, his former office manager, right?" Carlita asked.

"Correct, his former office manager and now loving wife," Jolly said with a smidgen of sarcasm.

CHAPTER FOUR

The instant the two sheriffs' deputies walked into the office, Tamra Fugit had a bad feeling. It was never a good omen for a private investigation outfit when law enforcement representatives unexpectedly came calling; her boss had advised her early on.

"Are you the office manager?" the stockier of the two asked.

"Yes," she answered from behind her desk, noting the moniker Luis Fernandez on his nametag. "What can I do for you?"

"We're looking for the whereabouts of a Mr. Adam Fraley whom we're informed operates this place," his partner asked, bearing the name Tommy Eanello.

"He's on vacation," Tamra said, leaving it at that.

Fernandez glanced at a notepad he had in hand. "Do you know where?" he asked in rote fashion.

"He's somewhere in Colorado visiting an acquaintance. However, I'm not sure exactly where he might be at the moment."

Fernandez's beeper went off. "Excuse me, I need to take a call in the squad car," he said. "Be back in a moment."

Tamra was hoping for a quiet holiday workweek, maybe even taking time off for a trip to the beach. It had been a while since she'd wiggled her toes in the sand. Like many transplants from up north, she spent an inordinate amount of time the first few years of her residence soaking in the sun and surf. As the years progressed, however, the weekly treks to the beach turned into monthly and ultimately annual ones. Meanwhile, sunbathing in the back yard had become a convenient substitute.

"Nice outfit you have on there," Eanello said, turning his roaming eyes on her.

Tamra casually smoothed her skirt over a crossed knee. "Thank you," she said demurely, wondering if the guy with the lean face and active eyes was oblivious to a woman's ability to distinguish between a look and a leer.

"Yellow's a good color for you," he said, perching himself on the edge of her desk. "It matches up well with your dark complexion."

Funny, she mused, how the exact same complimentary words spoken by two different men could be received in two entirely dissimilar ways. One thing for sure, it wouldn't take much to convince this guy to tear up a traffic ticket. She was fully expecting him to ask where he had seen her before when his partner returned, scrambling the would-be suitor from her desk.

"Can you tell us when Fraley will be back?" Fernandez asked.

"I'm not certain, sometime next week I believe," she said, continuing her evasiveness. She fancied whether Eanello was turned on by her hard-to-pinpoint posturing or by the way she filled out her clothes. "Can you tell me what this is all about?" she asked politely.

"We're not sure," Fernandez said. "We were sent here to find out where we could locate him."

Nobody seems to be sure about anything, Tamra concluded, which was the way she wanted it at the moment. They had yet to ask if she had a contact number, a question she fully expected and was unprepared to answer. She'd informed Adam early on in her tenure she preferred not to be placed in situations requiring her to tell an untruth. Bracing herself for the quandary to come, she caught a break when Jeff Blanchard, the building landlord, came waltzing through the door followed closely by his father, McKinley Blanchard. Their sudden entrance commanded center stage. The elder Blanchard, bent over and carrying a walking stick, peeked around the office as if he had stepped into the middle of a conspiracy. "Where's Fraley?" he barked.

"He's on vacation this week, Mr. Blanchard," Tamra responded politely.

"Are these two fellows working on my case," the old man asked, nodding in the direction of the two officers.

"No, they don't work for us. They're here on another matter," she said.

It wasn't McKinley Blanchard's stained straw hat nor his yellowish gray hair sprouting from beneath it, nor his hawk-shaped nose framed by beady green eyes that demanded everyone's attention. No, it was the long wool overcoat he was wearing in eighty-five-degree weather.

Fernandez gave up the effort in light of the old man's appearance. "Ma'am, if you hear from Fraley, give me a call," he said, handing her a calling card. Tamra took it, as well as one from his partner, favoring the deputies with an understanding smile, one that Eanello in particular appeared to appreciate.

"I hope whatever those cops are working on is not taking time away from my case," the elder Blanchard said, shedding his overcoat and throwing it over the back of a chair.

She had warned Adam about McKinley Blanchard's eccentricities. His son was continually relating them to her on his visits to the office, as though they were the spice of the son's life. How, for instance, his father at the age of eighty-eight was still umpiring little league baseball games, calling pitches balls or strikes before they were halfway to home plate, or how he remained active in the work force by placing ads in the paper for odd jobs, like the one offering rides to the airport for twenty bucks. For that one he had to spend a night in jail when nabbed by the police for operating without a business license. "He is the landlord's father," Adam had said upon taking McKinley's case. Whether his wife was actually trying to kill him, as he claimed, was secondary in importance.

"Now, where do we stand on my wife's plotting to kill me?" McKinley demanded of Tamra, who, given the encounter with the deputies, gladly reverted back to her normal flak-catcher role. "I'm sure Adam will review the case with you as soon as he's back from vacation," she said, striving mightily to humor the man.

"Come on, son. Let's get the hell out of here," McKinley snapped, grabbing the overcoat he had shed moments earlier. "I think I'll start my own private investigation business," he said on the way to the door. "There's still time to get an ad in the Sunday classifieds."

CHAPTER FIVE

La Gulch Cantina's interior décor was a study in shades of red and black, from its burgundy walls decked with rusted metal antique lights and checkerboard-tiled floors, to its mahogany leather furnishings and dark patterned servers' uniforms. In Adam's estimation, the dim atmosphere was more conducive to candlelight dinner trysts than light luncheon fare. But then, who was he to be passing judgment on restaurant design? His own uniform of the day, a Denver Broncos cap and oversized orange jersey borrowed from Reggie, was more appropriate for a living room couch than any eatery's ornate dining scheme.

Finishing off his last tortilla, Adam asked his server to summon the manager. He wanted to compliment the restaurant on the meal. From the corner booth at the far end of the rectangular room, he had a clear view of a separated bar area where the servers' station was located. Monitoring the station activities was a slender woman of moderate height with jet-black hair scraped to the back. She was dressed in a stylish charcoal-colored suit. Adam's server approached her to deliver the message. A minute later, the manager was standing at his side, a formal smile creasing her clear olive-skinned face. "I understand you wish to speak with me," she said with the slightest of Latin accents.

Adam glanced at the nametag. "Yes, Daniela. I wanted to compliment you and the staff for the fine lunch. I eat out quite often and I have to say I don't recall a better meal for the price."

She nodded her appreciation. "Thank you, sir. That is especially welcoming, coming from a Broncos fan."

For a split second, Adam missed the reference, forgetting his borrowed attire. "Oh," he exclaimed, doffing his cap. "Nothing like making it obvious. How about yourself? You a fan?"

She crossed her arms and shifted her weight to one side. "My husband has dragged me to a game or two. I'm much more of a soccer fan."

"How long have you lived in Colorado?" Adam asked.

"I was born in Mexico. I came here several years ago."

"What brought you to this area?"

She hunched her shoulders. "Land of opportunity—what else?"

"Have the opportunities presented themselves or is the restaurant business your chosen field?"

Before she could answer, Adam's server returned with the tab and another message for her boss. "There's a woman at the front entrance who says she needs to see you right away," she said, at the same time accepting Adam's credit card from his outstretched hand.

"Did she say what it is about?" Daniela asked.

"No, but she acts as if it's important."

Daniela turned to Adam. "Excuse me a minute."

The manager headed towards the foyer where a statuesque woman with wavy brown hair and dressed in an ankle-length skirt awaited her with a serious expression on her face. It was not the countenance of a saleswoman about to make a pitch, Adam observed. No, more like a legal or law enforcement representative bearing bad news. All at once, he wished the dark atmosphere of the place to be a shade darker.

Daniela listened attentively to the message at the conclusion of which the tall woman handed her a piece of paper before turning to leave. The manager glanced at the paper, let out a noticeable sigh and returned to engage again her appreciative customer.

"Bad news?" he asked, eyeing her change in demeanor.

"Not really," she replied, looking down at the paper in her hand, tapping it with the other. "The cops want us to be on the lookout for a guy."

"Dangerous type?"

"They want him for questioning."

"For what?" he asked boldly.

"Not sure," she said unconvincingly.

"They give a description?" he dared to ask, aware the manager's mind was elsewhere.

"Not much of one. Only that he is of medium size and from Florida."

Adam patted the front of his jersey. "I'm glad this is a Broncos jersey and not a Miami Dolphins one," he joshed, drawing a token smile. "Did they have a name?"

"Yes," she said, once more glancing at the sheet in her hand. "Adam Fraley."

Adam's server returned with his receipt and credit card. To his relief she laid them face up on the table in his direction and not Daniela's. He casually signed the receipt, handed it to the server, and snatched his credit card, sliding it into his back pocket.

"Well, I'd better get back and alert the staff to what's up," Daniela said, her distracted mind killing off the conversation. "Nice meeting you and hope to see you here again."

Adam was not sure what he would have done if Reggie had not come riding in on a white horse at that moment to rescue him from his predicament. In this instance, it was his white jeep, his arrival in the parking lot caught by Adam through one of the restaurant's dining room windows.

Adam scooted from the booth and stepped briskly to the exit, noting Daniela in conversation with the staff.

"Whoa!" Reggie exclaimed, managing to avoid a collision with him at the front entrance. "Sorry I'm late. The interview took much longer than I expected."

Adam laid a hand on the back of Reggie's shoulder, nudging him into an about face. "Let's get the hell out of here," he said.

"What? No lunch for me?" Reggie asked.

"I'll explain later or else you may be having your next meal behind bars with me," Adam said as they quick-stepped to the parking lot.

* * * *

"How the hell did they get your name?" Reggie asked, munching on a makeshift sandwich back at his kitchen table.

"I have no idea," Adam responded from across the table. "The reality is they do and that makes the trail much hotter for them and us."

"What was your take on Daniela?" Reggie asked between bites.

"Under the circumstances, impressions are all I can come up with."

"And those are?"

"She's professional in her appearance, sharp-eyed, and proper in manner—a company gal on the surface."

"In other words she had her game face on," Reggie said. "Anything lurking below the surface?"

"Her mind was distracted, which is understandable, considering the presence of the cop."

"Anything strike you about him?" Reggie asked, finishing off his sandwich.

"It was a she—tall, slim, and much like Daniela, professional in her manner."

Adam drummed his fingers on the table. "There is one other impression of Daniela I came away with," he said, almost as an afterthought.

"What's that?"

"She acted as though she was working below her station in life. You know, like all those people with graduate degrees waiting tables or driving cabs."

The telephone rang, booting Reggie from his chair to answer it. A moment later, he was holding the receiver out to Adam. "It's your office manager in Florida. She needs to speak with you."

Adam arched an eyebrow and took the receiver. "Tamra?"

"Adam, sorry to interrupt your vacation but I think you need to hear this. I had a visit from two sheriff's department deputies asking where you were and when you'd be back. I told them you were on vacation and should be returning sometime next week. They asked if you were vacationing in Colorado and I said yes, though I didn't specify exactly where. Do you know what this is all about? They wouldn't say, only that I was to tell you to contact them should I hear from you. I guess it didn't cross their minds to ask if I had a way of contacting you."

"Yeah, I know what it's all about. However, it's too involved to explain to you right now. If you hear from them again, try not to give them anything more until you hear back from me. Hopefully, everything will be resolved in the next few days. Can you do that?"

"Will do," she said. "Enjoy the rest of your vacation, if that's what it still is."

"Trouble on the home front?" Reggie asked.

"Trouble here has reached there." Adam stood and walked to the sliding glass door leading to the deck to gaze at the mountains. "Somehow they've identified me. Can't for the life of me figure out how," he said.

"It had to be through your plates," Reggie said. "I see no other way. Maybe someone around this complex sneaked a look without our knowing it."

Adam clamped his forehead with his hand. "The trucker!" he said, turning to face Reggie. "It was the trucker."

"Explain, please," Reggie said, lifting his gaze from the computer he was working at.

"As I was driving in during the Christmas Eve storm, I pulled off the highway onto the shoulder of the road to get my bearings. I parked in front of a trucker who obviously decided to wait out the storm, something I was considering as well. He wasted no time flashing his lights to let me know I was in his space. He may also have been suspicious of my intentions so he jotted down my plate number. I'm betting he called them in either right then and there or later, when he heard the alert going out for the red pickup with the Florida plates."

"So if it was the truck driver, it's a moot point now," Reggie said. "All it does is add urgency to making your case before you and I are boxed into a corner." Reaching into a wire basket on his desk, he pulled out a printed sheet of paper and handed it to Adam. "Here, this is an article my finance friend faxed me. It's a profile of Arlen Feldman that appeared in the Front Range Weekly before his legal troubles began. It may give you a little more background information on the guy."

Adam snatched the article from Reggie's hand and settled back into the kitchen chair to peruse the story. Accompanying the article was a full-length photo of Feldman presenting a fiscal conservative look—chiseled face—disciplined dark brown hair—creased gray flannel suit—

and black dress shoes. Above the article streamed the headline: *Money Man Finds Niche in Financial Windfalls.*

Carving out a niche in the financial arena can be a challenging task in a field saturated with specialists, but investment advisor Arlen Feldman did just that: he tailored Arlen Feldman Financial Management, Inc. to those upon whom fortune has smiled. With the surge in lotteries, sweepstakes, and the like, the fortunate few holding the winning hands are growing in numbers, something that has not escaped the attention of Feldman.

"People who are the beneficiaries of monetary windfalls are frequently individuals who, through no fault of their own, lack the basic understanding of how best to handle their newfound financial status," Feldman said. *"Unfortunately, the record shows many are unable to merge their lifestyle goals with their financial goals and end up back where they started before their unexpected gain. Our goal is to provide them the guidance to make the adjustment."*

When asked what advice his firm offers clients, Feldman underscored the need to reduce risk through a combination of wise budgeting and safe investing, primarily in secure corporate and government bonds. Asked how he came to choose investing as a vocation, he referred to a student field trip he took to Cripple Creek years ago to learn firsthand the story of the Colorado gold rush. It was there he was bit by the gold bug. "Holding a nugget of it in my hand was enough to give me the fever," he said. So why didn't he go into the buying and selling of gold? "I have in a modest sense," he said. "I recommend a small portion for each of my clients' portfolios, mainly as an insurance policy in case the entire financial system collapses as unlikely as that may be." Asked if that satisfies a client's desire for the precious metal, he answered, "It's paper gold, not the real stuff. One satisfies a need, the other satisfies a lust."

Feldman plans to expand his enterprise by opening a satellite office in Denver. To the question of whether he would ever consider giving up his firm's independent status by going public, he had a simple answer: "I like being my own boss." He is quick to point out whatever success he and his firm have achieved thus far is directly attributable to his wife Rita. "Without her support, I wouldn't be standing where I am today," he said. It takes a person of her understanding and patience to help guide you through the highs and lows of the entrepreneurial process.

Feldman Financial Management is one of many independent financial firms popping up along the eastern slopes...

Adam set the article aside and again looked out the glass door toward the distant mountain tops flushed with sunlight.

"Finished reading?" Reggie asked, noting Adam's contemplative pose.

"Yes…finished," he said, snapping out of his reverie.

"What'd you make of it?"

"Let me ask you something. The authorities were convinced Feldman bilked his clients but were unable to prove it largely for the reason they could not track down the stolen funds they were certain he accumulated over time. White-collar workers leave paper trails. White-collar criminals don't. Suppose he took the misappropriated funds and purchased gold, the hard stuff, not the paper kind, and hid it away— bought it in small enough amounts so as not to draw attention. Sound feasible?"

Reggie momentarily pondered the thought before nodding his agreement. "Sounds feasible. There are more than enough jewelry shops, pawnshops, and coin dealers between here and Denver for him to pull it off. Yeah, you may be onto something there," he said, warming to the idea.

"The question is how do we turn the speculation into fact?" Adam asked.

"I know a place to start," Reggie said with confidence.

"Where's that?"

"There's a guy who's a regular at the bar I tend. His name is Johnny Othello. He owns and operates a pawnshop called Johnny O's. It's southeast of here, right off I-25. We could pay him a visit—see what he thinks of your supposition. There's always the chance he may know of Feldman."

"A preferred customer, do you suppose?"

"Let's go find out," Reggie said, pushing himself away from the computer. "Better than being cooped up in here the remainder of the day."

* * * *

Johnny O's was a rectangular, stand-alone, red brick structure as nondescript as the strip shopping center it bordered. On entering the shop, the two visitors were greeted by the owner, a chubby, puffy-faced man wearing a visor and for whatever reason a white lab coat. Following a quick introduction, the three made their way through a maze of display cases, stands, and shelves, plus clusters of customers, to a spare back room furnished with a worn wooden table and chairs where the three settled in for a chat. Nice place for undercover deals, Adam mused while looking about. A no-smoking sign hung on one of the walls. Someone had scratched out the 'no,' which came as no surprise since the room reeked of cigarette fumes.

"I must confess. I'm surprised seeing you here, Reggie," the owner said in a thin, reedy voice. "What brings you to Johnny O's?"

"Business of a sort," Reggie replied, proceeding to relate to the proprietor Adam's theorem of a swindler converting his loot into a pot of gold by accumulating over time relatively small amounts of the stuff until the conversion was complete.

Johnny shrugged at the notion. "So as not to draw attention to himself—sure, as long as he has the pile stashed away in a place safe from prying eyes."

"Are all transactions on record?" Adam asked.

"You asking that in all seriousness?" Johnny responded.

It was Adam's turn to shrug.

"In all honesty the law is beginning to crack down on phantom transactions. For me to say the practice no longer exists would be misleading."

"So, single purchases of say around five K would not be considered unusual? Reggie asked.

"Not at all."

"Most gold is purchased in what form?" Adam asked.

"The biggest demand is for gold coins."

"So you would agree someone who doesn't wish to draw attention to himself is likely to choose this option?" Adam asked.

"If you're referring to someone like a swindler who is seeking to avoid a paper trail, yes. By the way, who is the swindler you have in mind?" he asked flat out. "You failed to mention his name."

Reggie looked to Adam as if this was his call.

"His name is Arlen Feldman," Adam stated.

Johnny nodded.

"You know him?" Adam asked.

The shop owner landed his gaze on Reggie. "From now on, everything is off the record, okay?"

Reggie glanced at Adam. "Sure," he said.

Johnny swung his attention back to Adam. "Yes. I know him, not on a personal basis but solely as an occasional customer."

"A buyer of gold?" Reggie asked.

"Yes, of gold coins. He claimed he was a hedge investor. As such, he considered it an insurance policy. He didn't trust the economy. He believed it was about to crumble, or so he said."

"Can you give us an estimate of his total purchases?" Adam asked.

"A dollar amount?" The proprietor gave the matter careful thought. "Altogether, twenty to twenty-five thousand."

"There must be at least fifty gold dealers between here and Denver," Reggie said. "If he made the rounds we're talking maybe a million or more in gold."

Johnny grinned his agreement.

"Are you aware of the financial fraud charges that were brought against Feldman?" Adam asked directly.

"Yes, later on, but if you think it would have mattered in our dealings with him, you would be mistaken. We operate in a don't-ask-don't-tell environment. It's the nature of the business."

"Is there any way we could verify Feldman was making the rounds?" Reggie asked. "Without us having to make them ourselves," he added with a coaxing smile.

"If you're willing to hang loose here for a few minutes, I can duck into my office across the hall and make some calls to verify if he was a pawn-hopper."

"We would appreciate that," Adam said, sending Johnny out the door.

47

"What are the chances the cops come busting through this door shortly?" Adam asked, half in jest.

"You know how it is, Adam. There are times in life you have to place your trust in people whom you know little of, if you're to get where you're going."

"How'd your job interview go?" Adam asked.

"Went well from my perspective," he said. "I could be back into the old trade before long."

"Reggie, did the authorities botch the Feldman fraud case?"

"From what I recall, I don't think so, unless you call a lack of evidence a failure on their part. Preston Marshall has a good reputation they say—tough and talented."

Adam rummaged through his mind. "Where have I heard that name before?" he asked.

"He's the DA who was handling the case," Reggie advised him.

"Any chance he will be handling the murder case?"

Reggie stood to stretch his arms. "A good chance I would say, considering the possible connection between the two."

With each passing minute, Adam's notion of the cops busting in did not seem far-fetched, despite Johnny's interest in maintaining a state of neutrality between the shop, the cops, and the customers.

At the twenty-minute mark, Johnny returned. "Your speculation is correct," he said. "He was making the rounds."

"That's all we need to know," Adam said. "Thanks much."

"Oh, there's one other bit of information brought to my attention you might be interested in," Johnny said, halting the two in their trek to the door.

"What's that," Reggie asked.

"At one of his shopping stops up in Denver he purchased a sturdy old chest. You know, the kind you can stash your treasure in."

* * * *

"I'm coming in from the cold, Reggie," Adam said, breaking the silence between the two on their drive home from Johnny O's.

"What do you mean you're coming in from the cold?" Reggie asked, briefly diverting his attention from the road to Adam. "You're turning yourself in?"

"Yes."

"For what reason?"

"Preston Marshall. I remember where I heard that name."

CHAPTER SIX

"Does the name Adam Fraley sound familiar to you?" Jolly asked.

"You brought me all the way down here to ask me that? No, never heard of the guy."

Arlen Feldman sat in the interview room with one arm slung over the back of his chair. His bored look provided Jolly a measure of satisfaction for he knew the guy sitting across the table from him and Carlita was far from bored. The wrinkles of concern surrounding his alert eyes gave him away. Agitated he may be. Disinterested, no.

"Let's start from the beginning," Jolly said. "Where and what were you doing the night your ex-wife was killed?"

Feldman freed his arm from the back of the chair and clasped his hands on the table. "I was home with my wife, spending a quiet Christmas Eve, enjoying a few glasses of wine, watching through the window the snow falling on the spruce trees, agreeing with my wife there was no better way to spend the evening," he said. "By the way, I don't drink and drive."

"You called your ex-wife on Christmas Eve?" Carlita asked, knowing the answer.

"Yes, to wish my kid a Merry Christmas."

"But you didn't speak to your child, correct?"

"My ex wouldn't put her on the phone."

"How often do you see Noelle?"

"Seldom, thanks again to my ex. She turned her against me. You know how it goes in those situations."

"Do you know who would want to kill your ex-wife?" Jolly asked.

"Lots of crazy people roaming the mountains, don't you know? Once they started closing down the mental hospitals, the inmates headed either for the streets or the hills. Wasn't there another killing in that region not so long ago?"

"Not that I'm aware of," Jolly answered.

"If you ask me, it's a beastly bearded thrill seeker," Feldman said in half-seriousness. "Beats any motive I would have." He straightened in his chair. "Look, I know it's the husband the spotlight is turned on first, but need I remind you, I'm no longer the husband. That part of my life is over with…settled in a court of law no less."

Carlita tapped her lips with a pencil before lowering it to make a note. "Police were called to your house by your ex on a couple of occasions for domestic abuse issues, were they not?" she asked.

"That was then," Feldman said. "You left out the important part. No charges were brought."

"Your child was present on each of those occasions, right?" she asked.

Feldman threw his hands out. "What's that got to do with Rita's death? Silly me, thinking I would not be harassed for a matter I had nothing to do with. I knew I should have brought a lawyer. You'd better start coming up with something more than me being the former husband or else I'll be filing harassment charges."

"Your present wife, Daniela—what sort of a relationship did she have with Rita?" Jolly asked.

"None, and why drag her into it?" he asked, invective pouring from his mouth. "Unlike Rita, she is a well-rounded, accomplished woman, multilingual and multi-talented. In addition to holding a degree in finance, she's a licensed pilot, registered interpreter, and great cook. Want me to go on?" he asked derisively. "Rita, on the other hand, had no interest in improving her lot in life."

"Maybe she was too busy being a mother," Carlita interjected, prompting a pause in the interview.

"Rita served as your office manager—correct?" Jolly asked, ending the brief silence.

"Something you already know, I'm sure."

"Was it Daniela's degree in finance that helped land her the job as Rita's replacement at Feldman Financial Management?" Jolly asked.

"Sure, along with other relevant qualities," Feldman said, the pupils of his eyes trending smaller by the word, as he strove to keep his anger under control. Jolly wondered if this was the same prelude to an explosion his ex-wife had witnessed the night of her death.

"Daniela comes prepared for job interviews," Feldman pointedly added. "It's what set her apart from the other applicants."

"We will need to talk to your wife if for no other reason than to verify your whereabouts on the night in question," Jolly said.

"Fine. Talk to her," Feldman bristled. "I have nothing to hide nor does she."

"So, the timeline is simple," Jolly said. "You spent the afternoon and evening at home. What time did you go to bed?"

A wry smile crept across Feldman's face. "Early. It's amazing what kind of mood a good bottle of vintage wine can put you in."

"How early?" Jolly asked, ignoring the lame attempt at levity.

"Around nine or so."

"And for the record, you not only spent the evening but the entire night at home."

"The entire day, the entire evening, and the entire night. There, does that cover everything?"

"Timeline wise, I'd say it covers everything from your point of view."

Feldman flashed a sardonic grin in Jolly's direction. "You don't like me, do you?"

The detective cast him a look as hard as granite. "Am I supposed to like you?" he responded.

"You're not supposed to dislike me, if I'm to be granted a level playing field."

"This isn't a game we're playing," Jolly pointed out.

"I agree. It's just that I keep seeing this image in my head of the scales of justice evenly balanced," Feldman said, leveling his hands in front of him. "Your personal feelings appear to be tipping the scales in one direction."

"That's for a judge or jury to decide," Jolly said, closing his

52

notebook to signal the end of the interview. "We'll be in touch in case we need further information."

* * * *

"Hear anything of import?" Jolly asked his partner in their post-interview confab.

"Nothing of great importance, though I thought it interesting he never asked how or where his daughter was," Carlita replied.

Jolly nodded his agreement. "As Feldman no doubt would say, a bad father does not a killer make."

"How much time do you figure it would take him to get from his house to his ex-wife's place?" Carlita asked.

"Less than an hour, even in the snow. That Land Rover of his has four-wheel drive and tires with enough traction to climb Pikes Peak in a blizzard."

"Now, if we only had a solid motive, clue, or lead to go on," Carlita said, crossing her arms in frustration.

Jolly folded his hands behind his neck. "I agree. Did you complete that background check on Daniela?"

Carlita flipped open her notebook. "Yes, though nothing jumped out at me. She immigrated to the states from Vera Cruz, Mexico several years ago at the age of twenty-one. She's the oldest of five children. All her siblings are still living in Vera Cruz. Her mother works as a cleaning lady. There is no mention of a father in any of the reports I could dig up."

Jolly unwrapped his hands from behind his neck. "He might have skipped out on the family," he suggested. "Sounds like the standard immigrant story. Someone comes here to make a living in order to help the family back home. How about you... did you come from an immigrant family?" he asked, putting on display his lack of the social graces.

"Didn't we all?" Carlita replied, ostensibly taking no offense to the question. "My father and mother came here from Cuba as part of the Mariel boat lift. They and their three children, including me, rode a cramped, rickety boat the entire ninety miles to Florida with our feet dangling over the side, hoping the sharks didn't take notice. Castro gave families joining the exodus virtually no time to prepare for the exit."

"How many refugees were there?" he asked.

"Over a hundred thousand, riding in boats of every description. Many of them broke down or ran out of fuel, which was the case with our boat. We had to paddle the last twenty miles to shore north of Miami where we were picked up by the U. S. Coast Guard."

"I hear Castro emptied his jails and mental institutions of inmates so they could join the flotilla," Jolly said, offering up a second observation ripe for misinterpretation.

"The criminals, outcasts, and outright gangsters made up a small portion of those fleeing," she said. "Many were from the professional class, like doctors and lawyers, whom Castro targeted as potential threats to his so-called peoples' revolution."

"They had to start over from scratch once they reached here?"

"Yes. Their degrees and licenses were of little use here. Some colleges honored the refugees' formal educations received in Cuba by allowing them to enter graduate programs in certain disciplines. My father was accepted into a master's program in library and information science. He ended up becoming a director of a small college library."

"Have you been back to Cuba?"

"No. I have no interest in returning, even for a visit. This is my home," she said with conviction.

Jolly nodded his understanding. "Sorry for the interruption. Now, back to Daniela."

Carlita checked her notes. "Okay, she worked her way through Mountain State College where she received her degree in finance. She then worked as an intern at a couple of financial houses before taking the job as office manager for Feldman's firm following Rita Feldman's leaving."

"If I recall right, she was there during the fraud case," Jolly noted.

"Yes. She came on board right before the civil case was filed, though there is no evidence she was involved in the illegalities. She has no prior criminal record."

"An innocent bystander?" Jolly asked.

"Appears so on the surface."

"Does the same hold true for Rita Feldman? What did you come up with on her?"

Carlita flipped through several more pages of her notebook. "As part of the divorce settlement, she was awarded custody of Noelle and child support. In addition, she was awarded the cabin. Turns out, Rita taught at the same small parochial school Noelle attended. She received a break in the tuition since she was a member in good standing of the parish where the school is located. Her job there allowed her to drive Noelle back and forth to school every day. Overall, her record as a teacher was exemplary. She consistently scored high in her evaluations. She also was well liked by her colleagues at the school. Not a bad word was said about her."

"Family? Boyfriends?" Jolly asked.

"Her parents are deceased. She had no siblings. According to her fellow instructors, she never mentioned any boyfriends nor was she seen at any of the school functions accompanied by one. Apparently, she devoted her entire life to her daughter."

"Was she financially solvent?" Jolly asked.

"Yes. She had no significant debt," Carlita said. "Must have ignored any advice her ex might have given her in this regard," she added, unwilling to avoid the dig.

Jolly smiled at the notion. "What's the back story on her leaving Feldman Financial Management?" he asked.

"From what I can tell, she wanted to get into teaching and when the opening came up at Noelle's school, she jumped at it. Whether she was privy to her husband's shady dealings is difficult to say. As with Daniela, there was no evidence she was involved in them. On the other hand, if she did become aware something was amiss it could have contributed to the marital breakup."

"She might have become aware of his dealings after she left," Jolly said.

"Yes, that's what I'm thinking. Also, the fact she left her position prior to Daniela coming on board could be significant. Why didn't she wait until her position was filled? The beginning of the school year was still months away, meaning she had time to hang around to train the new person. My guess is she either became aware of the financial fraud or of a personal relationship developing between her husband and Daniela.

Either way, she wanted to get out of there." Carlita interrupted her line of thought to give her partner a quizzical look. "Was Rita's roll or non-roll in all of this not considered during the fraud investigation?"

"Yes, but it's always nice to have a second opinion," he said. "So, from what you could determine, there were no demerits on her record."

"Correct, unless you want to count her marrying Arlen Feldman as one, which in itself is difficult to understand."

"Well, there are plenty of others he duped, including many so-called rational people," he said. "Unfortunately, conniving crosses personal and professional lines."

Jolly retrieved a stick of gum from his shirt pocket and slipped it into his mouth. "You're more the judge than I am in what I'm about to ask you, Carlita. Do Daniela and Feldman appear to be a match to you?"

"I'm not sure anyone is a match for Feldman, romantically speaking or otherwise. Even his smiles are laced with venom."

"I tell my daughters the first thing you look for in a man is whether he has a temper or not," Jolly said. "A calm demeanor is a long-term value. You can build a relationship on it. A hot temper can crumble it quickly. The problem is men are good at camouflaging it, even from an intelligent woman like Rita Feldman."

"I have a girlfriend who surreptitiously applies a temperament test to the men she's dating," Carlita said. "She will deliberately arrive late to an important dinner date, *accidentally* spill a drink on them, or take the opposite side of a political stance or, worst of all, switch the channel during a football game to determine their anger level."

"Not a bad idea," Jolly said. "She's thinking long-term."

"She's also still single," Carlita added with a spirited smile.

"What else have you got?" he asked.

"I called La Gulch Cantina and spoke with the owner, a man by the name of Bob Chandler. They do have a parking lot security camera in operation and we are welcome to view the tape."

"No court order required by them?"

"He said there was no need for one. They will cooperate fully."

"Is Daniela on duty today?"

"According to Chandler she is."

"Perfect. Let's make a visit."

* * * *

The combination of sunny skies, warmer temperatures, and post-holiday shopping bargains was enough to lure locals back onto city roadways lined with ash-colored snow shoved into mounds by overnight street crews. The change of the holiday season from family time to party time was in full swing. For cops it was not a changeover to celebrate. The respite from the street wars had ended, though in this particular season, it was 'the Christmas lull that never was' for Vernon Jolly and Carlita Perez.

By the time they arrived at La Gulch Cantina, Bob Chandler had the television monitor mounted on a mobile stand in his office and the tape queued. A wiry man with slick-backed hair the color of coal and eyes to match, he wore a tailored gray suit befitting his managerial role. "Here's the remote," he said, handing it to Jolly. "View to your heart's content. Let me know when you're finished."

"You mentioned over the phone Daniela is on duty today," Carlita said, as Chandler headed for the door.

"Yes, she is. Would you like to see her?"

"We'll let you know when," Jolly said, fingering the remote.

The relevant part of the tape was less than two minutes in length. It showed a man parking his white jeep in the lot and stepping toward the restaurant entrance where he disappeared out of camera range. A moment later, he reappeared accompanied by another man dressed in a Broncos' cap and jersey. They quickly drove away.

"Did you see Fraley when you were delivering the alert to Daniela," Jolly asked of Carlita.

"Yes, I do recall her talking to a customer in a Broncos' cap and jersey. I thought nothing of it at the time."

Jolly motioned to the monitor. "Recognize the big guy?"

"No, not at all."

Jolly rewound the tape and played it again. The path of the jeep prevented any view of the rear license plate. However, the path did take it right under the nose of the camera, allowing a clear view of a front plate proclaiming Jasper Jeep as the dealer of the vehicle.

"Let's bring Daniela into the conversation," Jolly said, prompting

Carlita to relay the word to the owner.

Daniela entered the room with a look of anticipation on her face. "You've viewed this tape?" Jolly asked as she took a seat at the table across from him.

"Yes, I helped Mr. Chandler set it up for you," she replied in a genteel tone.

"The man who was driving...he did not come into the restaurant?" Carlita asked.

"No, he did not."

"You spoke with Fraley while he was here?" Jolly asked.

"Yes, briefly. He asked to see me. He wanted to compliment the restaurant on the meal."

"Anything else?" Carlita asked.

"He asked how long I had worked at the restaurant and whether I wished to make this a career. That's about it. The conversation ended when you came in to see me," she said, nodding to Carlita.

Daniela was maintaining a proper decorum, but Jolly knew beneath the surface she was itching to know what this Fraley episode was all about. Since Carlita had already informed her Fraley was wanted for questioning regarding Rita Feldman's death, she certainly was aware of a connection, as vague as it appeared.

Jolly decided to ratchet up Daniela's concern. "Does your husband know Fraley?" he asked.

"No, I'm sure he doesn't," she said directly. "What exactly does this have to do with Rita's death?"

The interview had segued into a semi-interrogation, raising an obvious caution light in Daniela's eyes. She decided to run it. "My husband had nothing to do with Rita's death," she declared.

"I hope you understand, Daniela, we have to touch all bases in this investigation," Carlita said in a conciliatory tone.

Jolly wasted no time in jumping in with his follow-up. "You were with your husband the night she was murdered?"

"Yes, the entire night."

"Your husband briefed you on his interview with us, did he not?" Carlita asked.

"Yes, he mentioned it."

"He said you went to bed early…correct?" Jolly asked.

"Yes, around nine o'clock."

"You a sound sleeper?" Jolly asked, probing deeper.

"Not enough of one to miss my husband getting out of bed, if that's what you're driving at," she said, transitioning from a proper attitude to a perturbed one.

"How would you describe your husband's relationship with his ex-wife?" Carlita asked.

"There was no relationship," she stated firmly, signaling there was no need to pursue this line of questioning.

Jolly set aside the TV remote. "That's enough for today," he said. "Detective Perez and I need to make a visit to Jasper Jeep before the day's out."

All three rose to leave.

She's as puzzled and about as far away as we are from putting the pieces of the puzzle together, Jolly mused. Then again, maybe not.

* * * *

Jasper Jeep's showroom was in a festive mood in anticipation of the coming New Year. Multi-colored, giant balloons rose from its rooftop, gently swaying to the light breeze. Inside its oval interior scarlet ribbons and bows adorned the hoods of the latest model vehicles as sales personnel hovered about, prepared to intercept the next warm body displaying any inkling of interest in their product.

Into the gaiety strode Jolly and Carlita, making their way to the manager's desk while at the same time attempting to avoid eye contact with the gauntlet of sales staff. "Jack Carter, Manager" read the nameplate on the desk. Carter, a middle-aged man with clear facial features, a full head of dark brown hair parted in the middle and a serious countenance, looked up from a document he was studying to see a man and a woman looking down at him. He immediately glanced past them to his sales people as if to ask why the hell they hadn't intercepted these people. Jolly provided the answer, introducing himself, Carlita, and the reason for their visit. "We're trying to locate a missing man," he said. "All we know is that he purchased a new jeep from you."

"A '92?"

"Yes, a white one with your plate on the front," Carlita said.

Jolly was confident the man would cooperate. Businesses wanted to keep on the good side of the law. Citing privacy issues was the furthest thing from their mind when facing a cop. Furthermore, all he would be doing is lending a helping hand in their search for a missing person, which should be of no concern to him.

Carter shifted his attention to the computer screen. "The new cars went on sale in the fall, so there shouldn't be that many once we narrow them down. "Man? Woman? Hometown?" he asked, looking back up at them.

"A man, probably a local guy," Carlita said.

Carter continued to play with the keys and scroll the screen, every so often grabbing a pen off the desk to scribble a note. "Do you know if it is a trade-in?" he asked.

Jolly and Carlita glanced at each other. Both shook their heads.

"Well, in the few months they've been out, it appears we've sold three of the white models to men. Know what he looks like?"

"You have a description of the men on there?" Jolly asked in return.

"No, but I check all of the closing paperwork, so eventually I speak to them all."

"Big, bald, and brawny, with a full beard," Jolly said.

"Like he could fill a jeep front seat with no room to spare," Carlita added, drawing a wry look from her partner.

The manager leaned back and broke into a satisfied smile. "Your search then is over." He once more glanced at the screen and picked up pen and paper. "His name is Reginald Fielding. He lives in the Westside Condominium complex outside of Fort Carson. Here's his address and phone number," he said, handing over his notes.

The detectives decided to forego an advance call to Fielding in favor of a surprise visit in the hope of finding his fugitive pal. Locating the condos was a piece of cake, thanks to Carlita once having a girlfriend who lived there, the same one who was adept at testing a man's anger quotient. A half hour later, they were cruising the complex, looking for unit #2225. Carports ran parallel to the condos, separated by narrow driving lanes. The front end of the white jeep caught their attention first. It was parked alone in a doublewide shelter. Jolly pulled in next to it.

The two detectives walked to a cluster of mailboxes mounted next to the foot of a stairwell leading to the second floor. They noted the name R. Fielding on the box marked #2225. They climbed the stairs, knocked on the door and waited. When no one answered, they knocked a second and third time with the same result. Both detectives expressed their puzzlement. If the two were back out on the streets, why didn't they take the jeep? Were they roaming the roads in Fraley's truck, willing to risk recognition?

Back in their patrol car, Jolly radioed headquarters to alert them to the probability Fraley was out and about. "No need to send out another alert, detective," the voice on the other end responded. "Why's that?" Jolly asked. "Because Adam Fraley at the moment is sitting in your office waiting for your return."

CHAPTER SEVEN

"Mr. Fraley and Mr. Fielding. What brings you two fellows here?" Jolly asked from behind his desk, a power drink resting within arm's reach.

Adam noted the feigned indifference in the detective's deep voice. "I have a story to tell you, one I think may interest you, at least that's what I'm told by your desk sergeant out front."

"Let's hear it," Jolly said, taking a swig of his drink. "Start from the beginning."

"Before I begin, I have a question."

Jolly shrugged. "Fire away."

"How is Noelle?"

Jolly glanced at his partner sitting to the side of his desk.

"She's being taken care of," Carlita said. "She's in protective custody."

"Protective custody?" Adam asked of the woman he recognized from La Gulch Cantina.

"Child Services is in the process of finding her a foster home," Carlita explained.

Jolly turned to Adam. "Back to your story."

Adam related his tale of becoming lost in the Christmas Eve storm and ending up stranded in a mountain cabin with Noelle. "Needless to say, I was dumbfounded to find her home alone in those circumstances. It wasn't until I went to fetch some wood for the fireplace that I understood why."

"You left everything as you saw it?" Carlita asked.

"Yes...as is...as was."

"And you had no connection to Rita Feldman's death other than stumbling upon it in the aftermath?" Jolly asked.

"Correct," he said, aware of the prevailing skepticism.

"Then why did you leave?" came the follow-up from Jolly he was expecting.

"He doesn't care much for sitting on the sidelines," Reggie said from his seat next to Adam, prematurely jumping into the give and take.

"Bearing witness is not sitting on the sidelines," Carlita pointed out.

"It is by my measure," Adam countered.

"And what if she decided to go looking for her mother while you were sitting there in your truck?" she asked.

"I would have beat her to the shed," Adam pointedly responded.

"Okay, let's get back to what brought you here," Jolly said, impatiently tapping his pencil on the desk.

"Two items of information brought me here," Adam said, "one of which is hard information, the other speculative but potentially a game changer."

"Start with the hard stuff," Jolly said, his impatience showing.

"The night in question, as I was nearing the cabin, a guy came barreling toward me in the opposite direction. He was driving a Land Rover, the same make and color Arlen Feldman drives from what I understand."

"Did you get a look at the driver?" Carlita asked.

"No, he was by me in a flash, plus I was busy concentrating on what was ahead of me, not beside me."

"And the speculative item?" Jolly asked.

"Do you know a man by the name of Preston Marshall?" Adam asked in return.

Jolly thought for a moment. "Are you referring to the District Attorney?"

Adam continued with the back and forth questioning. "Was he involved in the investigation of the Arlen Feldman financial fraud case?"

"Yes, he was handling the case," Jolly said.

"At one point during my stay with Noelle, she was showing me some of the gifts under their Christmas tree, lifting them up one by one and reciting who they were intended for. One of them was for a guy named Preston Marshall, a person Noelle said she didn't know, which begs the question, what was the relationship between Marshall and Rita Feldman?"

Jolly looked to Clarita. "I'm sure there was no relationship other than a professional one between the two," she said. "Preston Marshall is a happily married man, if that's what you're driving at."

"In that case, why the present and more to the point, what's in it?"

"And where is it?" Reggie added, rubbing a hand over his beard.

Jolly again looked to his partner. "As far as I know, the crime scene has not been disturbed," she said.

"Woodshed and cabin?" Jolly asked.

"That's what the crime scene investigators last told me," Carlita said, "though I can't swear it's still the case. I doubt they confiscated the presents as evidence. If so, they could be stashed in the evidence room. It makes for a good question: should the intended recipients be made aware of their existence?"

Jolly folded his arms across his chest and addressed Adam directly "Tomorrow morning we'll visit the crime scene again. I'd like for you to tag along so we can compare notes."

"Fine with me," Adam said, relieved it wasn't a decision to take him into custody for his disappearing act. He reckoned it was like taking up a tax problem with the IRS. The first thing you hope for is an understanding if not sympathetic ear.

"Be here at eight in the morning," Jolly said, ending the meeting.

* * * *

"How come you didn't spring your gold-hoarding theory on them?" Reggie asked on the ride home.

"I was about to until Jolly cut things short," Adam said from behind the driver's wheel. "Have you heard anything regarding your job application?"

"No word yet. For now, I remain a barkeep by trade."

"What again is the name of the lounge you work at?"

"Barkers Lounge and Eatery. Say, Adam, Jolly made it clear from his body language and the directive he issued that it's you alone he wants tagging along with him tomorrow, not me."

"Hurt feelings?"

"Nope. All it means is I will be the one watching from the sidelines from now on. I'll be expecting updates, however."

"You think I should bow out also?" Adam asked, weaving his pickup in and out of heavy traffic.

"No, I think you should continue with what you're doing. Forget the vacation part. It's not like a juicier case is awaiting you when you get back home, right?"

Adam thought a moment before letting out a hearty laugh.

"Okay, what is awaiting you?" Reggie asked, "the case of the…fill in the blanks for me."

"The case of the resilient pacemaker," Adam said. "It's one of those you had wished you had never taken on, yet you had no choice, since the client is your landlord's father."

"The resilient pacemaker?"

"You got it. That's what my office manager dubbed it. The old man came shuffling into my office one day, claiming his wife of fifty years was trying to kill him. I told him to take it to the police but he already had to no avail. They dismissed it for lack of evidence."

"What evidence did he have?" Reggie asked.

"His evidence boiled down to this. His pacemaker is sensitive to magnetic fields. So, no MRI's for him or anything of the sort. In spite of this, his wife kept dragging him to the public library, which is equipped with a magnetic book theft detection system set up at the front entrance. Time after time she would lead him in and out of the library, as many as three or four times a day."

"All that going in and out and he didn't suspect something was up?"

"She was always ready with an excuse, like she forgot to get a book on her list, or she needed to use the restroom, or get her library card renewed."

"But no hard evidence?"

"The only hard evidence and what raised his suspicions were the pacemaker readouts he was receiving showing spikes in his heart rate that corresponded to his visits to the library."

"Where does the case stand now?"

"It's standing still, awaiting further evidence, which is unlikely to come."

"Headed for the cold case file," Reggie opined. "Years ago, I was involved in a case almost as strange, one that ended up making the local paper. A lady friend of mine took me on a mystery dinner train, one of those short runs where you eat, drink, and watch a play as you rock and roll along the tracks. Well, halfway through the play, we felt a big bump. Suddenly, the train and play came to a stop. Turns out it wasn't a piece of bad track or object of some kind, like a small boulder. No, it was the body of a middle-aged man, dead from having been run over by us."

"Part of the act?" Adam asked, maneuvering his pickup around a chuckhole.

"Yeah, that's what we were all thinking at the time, until the murmuring began among the cast members and crew, finally spreading to the audience. Before long, everyone realized the mystery aboard the train had been usurped by the riddle beneath it. It was later determined by the cops that the guy we hit was walking about under the influence and had passed out on the tracks."

"A play within a play," Adam said, guiding his truck through some thick slush and onto a street leading to the condo.

"Yeah, but that wasn't the end of it for me," Reggie continued. "A relative of the dead guy somehow got wind I was on the train and hired me as a citizen sleuth to look into it further."

"He suspected foul play?"

"Yes, but there was nothing I dug up to support his suspicions. On the contrary. The victim was a longtime lush and known to wander off into the night on drunken binges." Reggie paused to look across at Adam. "That's my strange one for the day," he said.

"Did you get your money back?"

"For the play being cut short?"

"Yes."

"It never occurred to me to ask for a refund. My mind was preoccupied with the circumstances surrounding what you call the play within the play."

No sooner had they arrived back at the condo than Adam's office manager was on the phone from Tampa.

"Tamra, what's up?"

"I thought I'd check to see if relations between you and local law enforcement out there have improved or should I brace myself for more calls?"

"Relations have improved considerably. Currently, I'm in good stead with them."

"There's another reason I wanted to touch base with you, Adam."

"I'm listening."

"It concerns McKinley Blanchard and his pacemaker."

"Oh yeah? I was just talking to Reggie about him a while ago. What's he up to?"

"He's not up to anything, Adam. He's dead. His pacemaker gave out. He passed away yesterday according to the landlord."

"I hesitate to ask where, but tell me anyway."

"In the public library."

"Please tell me he wasn't stretched out across the entranceway."

"Close to it, not across it, according to the landlord."

Adam attempted to choke down a chuckle but with limited success.

"Adam, it's not funny. He is the father of our landlord."

"You're right," he said, acknowledging her point. "Exactly how long ago did he die?"

"I don't know exactly when. What difference does it make?"

"Too late for a resurrection I'm afraid."

"And what does that mean?'

"I read a report a while back concerning an elderly man who, after he was pronounced dead at the hospice he was staying at, was transported to a funeral home. Five hours later, as they were preparing to embalm him, one of the workers noticed the body bag being kicked from the inside. It turns out the guy's pacemaker fired back up, bringing him back to life."

A moment of silence ensued on the line.

"Adam, I swear, if I hear a guffaw on the other end of this line, I'm going to start hoping whatever it is you're involved in up there winds up being a big red flag on your resume."

"Listen, Tamra. Mr. Blanchard led a full life and an exciting one, it appears."

"Adam!" she snapped. "I'm the one here having to deal with it."

"Seriously, turn everything we have on the case over to the cops. As far as we're concerned, it's a closed case."

"If the landlord asks anything regarding the status of the investigation, what am I to say?"

"Tell him what I told you. It's in the hands of the cops. We're done with it."

"Adam, are you sure things are okay on your end?"

"*Okay* is the right word to describe things here. Don't worry, I'll be home soon. I just can't say exactly when."

"Be safe."

"How often do you suppose Mr. Blanchard heard those words from his wife?"

"Adam, you're hopeless."

"Happy New Year, Tamra."

CHAPTER EIGHT

A leaden earth and sky greeted Adam and the two sheriff's detectives on their return to the cabin. No longer were the grounds aglow with ethereal holiday lights. Somebody had pulled the plug, underscoring the somber atmosphere. Moreover, falling temperatures had caused a hard crust to form on the surrounding snow cover, making the trek to the woodshed a cumbersome one. With heads bent to the wind and noses turning red, the three investigators stamped across the hardened surface to the small structure. It was Jolly's idea to first check the woodshed to compare notes with Adam.

"It's mandatory in this business for investigators to get their stories straight, or else it becomes divide and conquer time for defense attorneys," he advised.

Viewing the woodshed and its environs in the light of day, dim as it was, brought matters into perspective for not only Adam but for the two detectives as well.

"It would have taken some degree of upper body strength to haul her up by the rope," Jolly commented, looking up at the shed's crossbar. "Perpetrated by a man, it's safe to say."

"Might there have been an accomplice?" Carlita asked.

"Possible," Jolly said. "After all, we haven't officially ruled out Fraley here."

Carlita cast a soft smile Adam's way on hearing the comment. "Did the killer strangle her inside or outside?" she asked.

"Chances are it was in here," Jolly said, stepping inside the open door, "particularly if they were in the middle of a heated quarrel. No question the mother would have wanted to keep it beyond earshot of the child. What do you think, Fraley?"

The question caught Adam off guard, not its content but the fact Jolly had directed it at him. "My guess is Feldman called his ex-wife earlier in the evening as we've learned and demanded to see her. They met back here and the fireworks started for any number of reasons.

"Care to list them in order of likelihood?" Jolly asked while pacing the woodshed's interior to look for something out of the ordinary.

"You go first," Adam said, drawing a smile from the veteran detective.

"No ligature was found from what I understand," Carlita said. "He no doubt took it with him or tossed it who knows where."

"Difficult item to find," Jolly commented. "It could be buried in the snow but I'm not inclined to wait around for a complete thaw to make certain. You notice anything missing from the night in question, Fraley?"

"Other than a dead body, the stretch of rope it was hanging from, and the armful of logs I hauled away, all appears the same."

Jolly slapped his gloved hands together. "Okay, let's go find Preston Marshall's Christmas gift."

Entering the cabin once again, Adam was reminded of the old saying that a house is a place, a home is a person. The electrical power to the cabin remained on; nonetheless, its energy was completely drained. Pausing at the entranceway to take in the interior scene, his attention immediately drew not to the presents under the darkened tree but to the couch where Noelle's blanket still lay crumpled. This is as much a crime scene as the woodshed, he said to himself. From the corner of his eye, he caught Clarita from across the room watching him observe the couch and the blanket. She favored him with an understanding smile.

"Here's Preston Marshall's gift," Jolly announced from his bent position beneath the tree, holding the present high for them to see. "Let's take a look-see," he said, coming out of his crouch with great effort.

They followed him to the kitchen table where he handed the present, no bigger than an oversized envelope, to Carlita. "I'll let you have the honor," he said.

She accepted it hesitantly. "Did you receive Mr. Marshall's

permission to open it?" she asked.

"I called him and he gave the okay," Jolly said. "He had no idea what it could be. Hell, I had to remind him who Rita Feldman was."

Carlita opened the package. It contained a small manila envelope. From inside it she retrieved a folded, letter-sized sheet of paper. Fingering it open, she studied the contents for a minute before handing it back to Jolly, who in turn examined it. When finished he handed it across the table to Adam for his perusal. What Adam saw gave meaning to the blank expressions on his tablemates' faces. Drawn on the sheet was a double horizontal line. It represented a road running east and west. Midway through the line was a scratching indicating a bridge. The letters RG appeared above it. Five miles west of the bridge and two miles north of the road, so marked, was sketched a stand of trees. Aside the cluster of trees was scribbled the letter X.

"Either of you have any idea what these scribbles indicate other than the location of buried treasure?" Jolly jokingly asked.

Adam laid the opened sheet on the table. "That's exactly what they're indicating," he said. Having grabbed their full attention, he went on to relate his hoarding gold theory, explaining how Feldman used the stolen funds he raked off his clients' portfolios to purchase pieces of gold from myriad dealers and how he bought a chest to store them in, presumably to stash the loot away.

"How much gold are we talking about?" Jolly asked.

"Could be anywhere from a half million to over a million," Adam said. "You can carry twenty-thousand bucks' worth of gold in a single pocket of yours. Think what you can stash in a chest."

The two detectives stared at the map with something akin to a newfound reverence.

"Unbeknownst to Rita Feldman?" Carlita asked, breaking the momentary silence.

"Maybe or maybe not," Adam responded. "Correct me if I'm wrong, Detective Jolly, but from what I gather, Rita Feldman was never considered an accomplice in the fraud case against her ex-husband."

"True. There was no hard evidence she was involved," Jolly said. "Whether she got wind of it at some point is another matter."

"I don't believe she was named as a defendant nor called as a witness in the civil case," Carlita said.

"Nonetheless, she must have had her suspicions," Adam said. "By chance or by guile, somewhere along the line she came up with this map, which reinforced those suspicions. My guess is she brought the matter of the map to her ex-husband's attention or else he somehow became aware it was in her possession. Whatever the exact circumstances, she posed an imminent threat to him. This led to the heightening of hostility between the two culminating in the Christmas Eve confrontation. He called demanding to see her in person, probably to convince her to turn over the map. He may have couched it in terms of wanting to see his daughter. After all, it was Christmas Eve. She relented, met him in the back and refused to turn over the map. In fact, she already had packaged it as a present to Mr. Marshall, something Arlen Feldman was unaware of when he took her life."

"Why would she let him know the map was in her possession?" Carlita asked.

"I wondered that myself," Adam said, "and my answer is she let him know it for the pure satisfaction of saying to his face 'I was right all along about you and your dealings.'"

Carlita picked up the map and took a second look. "It appears to be the original and not a copy."

"Which is not to say there are no duplicates," Jolly pointed out. "Would you say those are markings made by a male?"

"Not much to go on," Carlita said, "but yes, they look to be markings made by a male."

"Anyone know what the RG stands for?" Adam asked.

"Royal Gorge," Jolly said. "If your conjecture is correct, Fraley, Feldman buried his treasure trove seven miles west-northwest of the bridge. The problem is the map is far from precise. Feldman probably scribbled it as a reminder of the general vicinity where he left it. There are no distances indicated between the X and nearby points. He may know the exact location of the trove but anyone else would have to dig up an entire section of land with no guarantee of finding it."

"I suppose the best place for people to hide their gold is underground," Carlita said. "It seems a natural choice, especially if it is a large amount."

"What about a metal detector?" Adam asked. "It might save time and effort."

"Yes, they can be a worry for gold hoarders," Jolly said. "However, if you bury it deep enough or behind metal decoys, you can escape detection. The only sure way of finding it is digging it up. I'm sure Feldman was aware of this and took precautions to see that his loot was safely tucked away, or else he doesn't have as much precious metal sense as he thinks he has."

"You'd think a financial advisor would be all in favor of diversification," Adam jested. "You know, hiding portions of it under the mattress, behind the washing machine, inside fake books, or in the backyard."

"I read during the depression people would hide their cash in nearly anything around the house—behind paintings, under floorboards, between pages of books, in tin cans buried in the yard," Clarita said, "every place but the bank."

"The banks had gone under," Adam said. "I'm not even sure banks today are the safest place to stash away your gold. A white-collar crook changes a few numerical figures and your gold disappears into somebody else's account. On the other hand, a thief goes looking for buried treasure in your backyard and he has to get past your shotgun. Which is the surest method of storage?" he asked. "As I understand it, the key is to keep people from knowing you have gold in the first place. In that scenario, it doesn't exist."

"A finance guy who was trying to sell me some of the stuff assured me physical gold is the most private investment you can make," Jolly said. "Not even the Internal Revenue Service knows you have it in your possession."

"Why not install a large safe for it?" Carlita asked. "You can have it installed without anyone knowing."

"Except for the installers knowing," Jolly countered. "Like Fraley said, the key is not letting anyone know you have the gold, which is what Feldman was attempting to do."

Jolly exhaled a deep breath before continuing. "Here's what I propose. Feldman needs to be flushed out. The map gives us the opportunity to do it. Carlita, see if you can set up another meeting with

Daniela, tomorrow if possible. Let her know it's an urgent matter. She may bring a lawyer but that's okay. What we'll do at the meeting is inform her additional information has come to our attention that implicates her husband in the financial fraud matter as well as the murder case. We tell her we have solid evidence her husband has been hoarding gold paid for with stolen funds. We do not tell her we know where the gold is hidden. At this point, we ask her cooperation in determining its location. It's highly unlikely she will agree to cooperate. Nevertheless, by reporting back to him what we told her, it could spur him into grabbing the gold and making a dash for it. Otherwise, even if we did manage to locate the exact spot where it's hidden and dig it up, he would simply deny it was his map and his haul. We would end up having the prize but not the perpetrator. Of course, should he bite, we will have a tail on him. What do you think? Worth a try?"

Carlita looked to Adam, inviting his input. "Whether she is on her husband's side or not, I agree she is sure to bring the matter up with him, making it likely he will act on the information."

Both men turned to Carlita. "I agree," she said. "Turning up the heat may rouse him into action."

"I do have a request," Adam said.

Jolly tucked the map into his shirt pocket. "Let's hear it."

"I'd like to be part of the investigation."

"You are a part of the investigation," Jolly replied.

"As it goes forward," Adam quickly added.

In the brief time he had known him, Adam judged Jolly to be a skilled detective whose experience served him well. He was not the type to lose sight of the goal. Whatever it took to solve the case, he was willing to consider, as long as it didn't threaten the integrity of the investigation or violate legal boundaries. As the lead detective, there was no question he had significant discretion in conducting the case.

"Consider yourself a tag-along witness to what transpires from here on in," Jolly said, "a citizen observer so to speak with no law enforcement authority. You okay with that, Carlita?" he asked, wisely running it by his partner.

"Fine by me," she said.

Departing the cabin Adam took a final look around at the haunting images. "What will be done with the presents?" he asked.

"Good question," Jolly said, leading the exit out to the car. "At the moment, they are in legal limbo."

Adam wondered if this was the stuff of urban legend. For others it may well be, he concluded. For him it was all about a murder, an elusive motive, and a little girl whose world had vanished into a black hole.

* * * *

"Missed out on the job," Reggie announced to his guest upon his return.

"Sorry to hear that," Adam said, settling into a kitchen chair across from him. "There'll be other opportunities, I'm sure."

"They seem to be dwindling by the day."

"Why don't you get back into the private eye business where you answer to yourself and not to others? It seems a better fit for you."

"Not to sound trite, but been there, done that," Reggie said dismissively. "I'm aiming for a more structural and stable working environment—a steady paycheck to be specific."

"Are you making enough to keep your head above water?"

"Yeah, the tips keep me afloat. If not for them, I would have gone under by now."

"I understand the bar business can get into your blood," Adam said. "People working it end up bouncing from one watering hole to another, like the customers themselves."

"What job doesn't get into your blood if you're associated with it for any length of time?" Reggie said with resignation. "The question is whether it stirs up the bad or good blood in you."

"Big New Year's Eve coming up at Barkers Lounge and Eatery?" Adam asked.

"Yep. As a matter of fact, it'll be a doubleheader for me. Following my regular shift, I'll be serving drinks at an all-night private party, which reminds me to tell you I won't be seeing you until sometime later in the day."

"Can you sleep on your feet?" Adam cracked.

"You mean can I sleep on my feet and serve drinks at the same time? No, but like I said, the tips keep me awake, especially at the private functions. It's a lucrative gig. Want to drop by?" he asked, knowing the answer to come.

"As you're aware, Reggie, I'm the last guy you want to invite to a party."

"If I recall right, you occasionally hit the clubs in your younger days."

"Sitting in a club is different from working the floor at a party. In a club, you don't feel obligated to go around and meet people. You can simply sit and observe all by your lonesome while enjoying a drink and the music."

"No wonder you're still a bachelor. If I had half your looks, I'd be flashing them to whomever, wherever, and whenever I had the chance. By the way, what did Preston Marshall's present turn out to be?"

"Present?" Adam said, missing the reference for a moment. "Oh yeah, it was a map."

"A map? Santa must not have been in a jolly mood."

"Yes, it was a sketchy map scribbled, we think, by Arlen Feldman, indicating he may have buried the gold somewhere near the Royal Gorge bridge. It's not specific as to where."

"Are the cops going to go looking for it?"

"No. They're hoping Feldman will lead them to the exact spot, and then nab him with the goods."

"How do they plan on getting him to do that? He's not going to voluntarily lead them to it or else he's not as clever as everyone seems to think he is."

"By getting word to him through his wife that the map has come into their possession. It should flush him out if he thinks his cache is about to be unearthed."

"What's your role in all of this?"

"Citizen Observer."

"Sounds like another one of those manufactured titles governments are good at handing out," Reggie said. "Are you a good observer, Adam?"

"A good observer, but a better listener." Which should suit his new role nicely, he mused.

* * * *

Out of her formal restaurant uniform, Daniela Diaz presented an even more striking presence. A combination ruffled white blouse and light blue pleated skirt highlighted her naturally dark skin and raven hair she had loosened to the shoulders. Still, her formal demeanor remained intact, though a glint of surprise appeared in her eyes on seeing Adam sitting aside the two sheriff's detectives in the interview room. She had to be asking herself, "What the hell is he doing here?" Adam thought, as well as questioning her decision to come without consul. Undoubtedly, it would be the last interview without her lawyer present, he surmised.

As it turned out, it was less an interview than an update. Jolly gave her the reason for calling her in, citing the new piece of evidence in the form of the map that had come into their hands. "It confirms your husband's involvement not only in the financial fraud case but in his ex-wife's murder," he said.

At first, Daniela reacted to the news as if told the world was round. When informed by Jolly of the consequences of her stance, cracks in her demeanor slowly appeared. Tears welled in her eyes, betraying her steely resolve. Understandably, Adam believed. Her American dream was close to crumbling. The question confronting her was whether she should ride it out with the man she had hitched her wagon to or cooperate with authorities and keep her dream alive. Jolly didn't make it easier for her by stating this was her final opportunity to come on board. In what manner he didn't say, though it went without saying it was her ability to bust her husband's Christmas Eve alibi that was of greatest interest to him. "I know much of what has transpired occurred before you came on the scene," Jolly said, "and I can understand you wanting to stand by your husband. However, we have an investigation to complete and you are either with us or against us in that regard." Jolly paused to await a response. It never came. "You know how to get in touch with us in case you change your mind," he said, closing the session.

"Did you two find it strange she didn't ask to see the map?" Carlita would later ask.

They both concurred. Jolly, however, refused to say whether he would have acquiesced to the request. "Let's face it, though we may have planted a burr, the entire conversation proved to be unenlightening," he said. "On a far different matter, when I spoke to Preston Marshall earlier, he informed me he wants to meet with the sheriff and me to go over the case."

"He's starting to feel the pressure from the press and public?" Adam asked.

"No doubt, which means he's going to pass it on down the ladder. District attorneys are all about wins and losses."

"And we aren't?" Carlita asked, displaying a skepticism.

"We're about catching criminals. They're about convicting them, which is why they are hung up on technicalities," Jolly said. "They're terrified of them. Nothing could suit them better than to be handed a nice clean case. Otherwise they enter into plea agreements with the greatest of ease."

What they all agreed on was that the investigation had reached a momentary impasse. Still, there was all that yellow metal out there to keep the pot boiling.

* * * *

Preston Marshall rose from behind his mahogany desk to greet the two sheriff's department representatives. "Sheriff Collins, Detective Jolly, have a seat," he said, motioning to twin upholstered chairs fronting his desk. In Jolly's eyes, Marshall was the dapper DA, invariably attired in one of his many pinstriped suits, tailored tight to his medium build frame. Today, he wore a black and white pinstripe to go with his enameled black hair that was fast turning white at the temples.

"I thought it time for a briefing on the Feldman case, Sheriff," Marshall said in a clear voice. We're beginning to receive significant blowback from the public regarding the case. Many of the inquiries are coming from victims in the financial fraud matter. Others are asking if Feldman's getting away with murder this time. On top of that, the press is starting to poke around with greater frequency, sensing something big is in the works. I don't wish to mislead them, particularly after the PR beating we took in the first case." Marshall leaned back in his chair and clasped his finely manicured hands behind his neck. "So, Albie, bring me up to date."

Jolly had come to know Sheriff Albie Collins, a lanky, raw-boned man to be a fair, uncomplicated individual whose physical presence belied his tough nature. His supervisory style was simple. He would provide you sufficient resources and free rein to get the job done, and you'd best get it done or you'd be back to handing out parking tickets. "Be forewarned," a colleague once advised Jolly, "excuses are as dangerous as hand grenades when thrown at him."

The sheriff proceeded to outline the progress of the case, obviously trying not to raise or lower expectations regarding the eventual outcome. Pragmatic he also was.

"Sounds as if the gold matter is central to the case," Marshall said. "What are the odds of recovering it?"

The sheriff looked to Jolly. "As it stands now, I'd say fifty-fifty, though that may be on the optimistic side," the detective answered.

"This private detective who's been assisting you—Adam Fraley I believe is his name. I'm not sure if it's a good idea having him on board," Marshall said. "Is his presence crucial to the case?"

"To this point it has been," Jolly quickly said. "It was his gold idea and discovery of the map that opened things up."

"The problem is defense attorneys could have a field day if somehow he screws things up," Marshall pointed out.

Here we go with the technicalities, Jolly mused.

"At the moment, we have him on board as a Citizen Observer," the sheriff said. "I know that's a stretch but we feel we're getting close to a resolution and would hate to change horses in mid-stream."

"You agree with that assessment, Detective Jolly?"

"I agree."

"Okay," Marshall said, unclasping his hands from the back of his neck. "No one wants to crack this case open more than I do. In my dealings with Rita Feldman, I found her to be an honorable woman. If anyone deserves justice, it is she, even if it is delivered posthumously. However, there are legal parameters we must observe if we are to avoid putting the case at risk. I strongly recommend that if the case has not come to a resolution within a week, you release Mr. Fraley back into the civilian world. He poses too much of a risk, I'm afraid."

The sheriff and Jolly exchanged glances, both nodding their

79

understanding.

CHAPTER NINE

From the entrance road a half mile away, the big red barn stood tall amid the sprawling flatlands of eastern El Paso County. Some years back, in a moment of civic contribution, George and Elaine Jansen, family farm operators and parents of a special needs child, decided to convert the barn into a petting zoo for the youth of the region, in particular disadvantaged and disabled youth. For Carlita Perez the attraction soon became a favorite destination for the groups of youngsters she would take on outings in her limited spare time. On this afternoon, she had in tow but one child, deciding the special circumstances warranted it.

Near the entrance of the barn was a kiosk with a sign above it stating, "Don't feed a finger, feed a cup of grain." In addition to the grain, the kiosk offered fresh eggs and milk for sale. Carlita and her charge opted to forego the feeding and stick to the petting.

Heated to a comfortable degree, the interior of the barn was partitioned off by a series of closed pens, each housing a pair of animals in Noah's Ark style. Goats, ducks, chickens, miniature horses, potbellied pigs, rabbits, donkeys, and sheep were all represented. Into the mix of circling kids and accompanying adults walked Carlita and her companion, holding tight to her hand.

"Do you have a favorite animal?" Carlita asked.

"I like the horses," Noelle said. "My mother promised to get me one when I got older."

Carlita led her to the horse pen where a child with Down Syndrome was hugging one of the miniatures around its outstretched neck with all his might. Noelle gently stroked the mane of the companion horse. "I wonder what his name is. Do you know?" she asked of her escort.

"I don't know, but your question brings up a good idea. I'll suggest to the owner they put the names of the animals on the pens."

They strolled from pen to pen, mingling with the other children, listening to the neighing, snorting, clucking, and myriad of other sounds emanating from the enclosures. Along the way Noelle would suggest names for the animals, invariably basing them on a physical feature— Nosy, Spotty, Fatty, and the like. In a brief moment of mirth, she christened one of the ducks 'Adam.'

"Why that name?" Carlita asked.

"They have the same brown eyes," she said.

"I see. I'm glad it's not because he quacks like a duck."

"Why are the goats called kids, the same as us?" Noelle asked at the next stop.

"You ask tough questions, young lady. I don't know. I suppose it's been that way for centuries."

Once the circle of the arena was completed, Carlita led Noelle to an empty bench off to the side of the barn, out of the way of foot traffic. "Let's take a break," she said, knowing it was anything but a break she had in mind. The break was in the simple stroking and touching of an animal that induced a calming effect. Much like a household pet, they had a way of accepting people for who they were. In so doing, they epitomized the concept of unconditional love. Her experience in dealing with traumatized children taught her the worst approach to recovery was to ignore the underlying cause of the trauma, hoping that it would eventually fade away. Carlita was not one to let things fester, especially when it came to post-traumatic disorder in children. She learned long ago that before the healing begins, the processing of the event in the child's mind must occur. For Noelle to escape out from under the shadow of her mother's death, she would first have to come to terms with it.

"How have you been feeling?" she asked her charge.

"Oh, okay."

"You miss your mother, don't you?"

"Yes," she said, digging her hands into her jacket pockets.

A large group of chattering children and their supervisors filed past them, momentarily interrupting the conversation.

Alone once again with their thoughts, Carlita got the question she half-expected and fully welcomed. "Did my father kill my mother?" Noelle asked, raising her eyes to her in inquisitive fashion.

"We believe he did, honey."

"Why?"

"Nobody knows for sure," Carlita said. "There are no easy answers as to why he did it other than he is a very sick man. One thing is certain. He had no good reason to take her life. You must always remember, your mother was a good woman and a wonderful mother to you. She did not deserve to die."

"You said he was a sick man. Is he still sick?"

"Yes, he is still a very sick man."

"Will he get better?"

"No one knows the answer to that question. We'll just have to wait and see."

Carlita could see clearly the confusion forming in Noelle's eyes, along with the forming of tears. "It's kind of scary, isn't it?"

Noelle nodded her agreement.

Carlita allowed her a few moments to digest the situation before continuing. "Tell me what you're thinking," she said, giving her a light squeeze of the hand.

"I don't know. What's going to happen to me, I guess."

"I'll tell you what's going to happen to you, Noelle. You're going to grow up to be the woman your mother always wanted you to be," she said with firmness.

"Who's going to take care of me?"

"There'll always be someone there to take care of you, honey. Don't worry. I promise you from now on things will get better. Okay?"

"Okay."

Who in the world could blame her, if her childlike faith in people was broken? Carlita asked herself. *Yes. Restoring it likely would be a long process but therein lies the mystery of faith*, she supposed. *It may lie dormant, but it never dies.*

For a while longer, they watched the strings of spirited children flow past them, happy faces on parade for a pair of not-so-happy ones.

Finally, Carlita looked down at her charge. "Ready to go?" she asked.

Noelle nodded, her hand still clinging tightly to that of her escort.

CHAPTER TEN

Adam awoke New Year's Day to a ringing in his ears, not from an alarm clock, nor a night out on the town, but from a phone located on a nightstand adjacent to his bed. He fumbled for the receiver, expecting Reggie on the other end of the line. Instead, it was Jolly. "If you want to go along for the ride, you've got a half hour at most to make it to the truck stop right off the Fountain exit on I-25 South," he barked. "Our stakeout man says Arlen Feldman is on the move." Before Adam could respond, the line went dead.

He jumped into his clothes and into his pickup. Ten minutes later he was headed south on the interstate, pushing the speed limit. Twenty minutes further along, he spotted the Fountain exit. Hurrying down the off ramp, he swerved his pickup into the truck stop parking lot, narrowly missing an outward-bound eighteen-wheeler. He pulled to a stop to survey the scene. Jolly was nowhere in sight, leading him to believe he had missed his ride. The honk of a horn drew his attention to a utility truck parked several slots away. "Get your rear over here," Jolly yelled through its lowered driver's side window.

Adam hustled over to the truck and hopped into the cab next to Carlita who had scooted over to make room for him. She was in jeans, he noted, more in style with the blue-collar role she was playing. In her hand, she held a third hard hat, which she handed to him. He obligingly donned it, a misfit though it was. He had heard of cops utilizing utility vehicles instead of unmarked cars as a surveillance tactic. The former could easily be identified by lawbreakers and law adherents alike. *Not a bad idea*, he thought, *particularly if you're headed out onto rural roads where utility trucks draw less attention.*

"Feldman's about ten miles north of us and headed our way, according to our stakeout guy," Jolly said. "We're still waiting on an answer to why he didn't take State Highway 115, a more direct route," Carlita added.

The answer arrived immediately over the two-way radio fitted into the cab. "Large sections of the state road are under repair," the even-toned female voice reported. "Could be the reason he's taking the longer route."

"Let's hope that's the case," Jolly responded, "or else this is all for naught."

"How far do you plan on trailing him?" Adam asked.

"At least to the intersection with Highway 50," Jolly said. "If he's headed for the Royal Gorge, he'll have to turn west at the juncture."

"He's presently about three miles behind you," the voice crackled over the radio.

Jolly cranked the utility truck's engine and eased the vehicle out of the parking lot and toward the interstate's on-ramp.

"You're not going to wait until he passes?" Carlita asked.

"Best to start out ahead of him," Jolly said, maneuvering the truck onto the highway. "In his mind we're simply another utility crew headed out on a job. Pulling in behind him might put us on his radar."

Adam kept his eyes fastened to the side mirror while Carlita focused on the middle rearview. Meanwhile, traffic was light, allowing Jolly to sneak peeks at the driver's side mirror without fear of rear-ending someone.

"He's coming into view," Adam said, spotting the Land Rover less than a quarter mile behind them.

"See him yet?" the voice crackled over the radio.

"He's in sight," Carlita responded.

"Then he's all yours," the voice said. "Keep us informed."

"Try and avoid any eye contact," Jolly advised his companions.

Feldman closed from the rear, flipped on his left blinker, and commenced to pass them.

Jolly kept a reasonable distance behind the suspect once he had made his pass, sufficient to allow several other cars to dodge in and out from between them.

"He doesn't appear to be in any hurry," Carlita observed.

The question dogged them all along the way as to whether Feldman intended to turn west on Highway 50 or continue south on I-25 to who knew where. As they neared the intersection, all eyes locked on the Land Rover's rear orbs.

"Come on…come on," Jolly whispered aloud, urging the right blinker to come alive. A few yards from the exit ramp, it did as urged, easing the anxiety within the cab.

Jolly followed the Land Rover onto Highway 50, heading west up the slopes toward Canon City and the Royal Gorge turnoff forty-five miles in the distance.

"Ever been to the Royal Gorge, Fraley?" Jolly asked, settling into his tailing routine.

"Not only have I never been there, I'd never heard of it until that map showed up."

"This will be a first for me," Jolly said. "How about you, Carlita? "Been there, done that?"

"I've been over it and under it," she said.

"Explain to our volunteer here what you mean by that," Jolly said.

Carlita glanced at Adam. "The gorge is extremely narrow. The floor of the canyon is only fifty feet wide or so on the average. It's several hundred feet wide at the top. The drop to the bottom is over a thousand feet. You can travel over it by way of the bridge that spans it or travel the bottom of it by rail. I've done both. You can also travel the canyon floor by raft, which I've never done nor plan to do."

"Fifty feet at the bottom doesn't leave much room," Adam said.

"Enough room for the railroad tracks and the Arkansas River, which is to the Rockies what the Colorado River is to the Grand Canyon," Carlita said.

"So, from the way you describe it, we're about to see a giant gash in the ground with a sliver of a bridge spanning," Jolly said.

"You could put it in those terms," Carlita said in a dismissive tone, indicating her preference for the grander vision.

"Which is the better route—over or under it?" Adam asked.

"I'd say if you're the adventurous sort, take the bridge. It's little more than a series of wood planks laid over a steel bed."

"How wide and how long?" Adam asked.

"About eighteen feet wide and twelve hundred feet long," she said. "The entire bridge can rumble and sway depending on the amount of traffic and wind gusts. It's generally regarded as the world's tallest suspension bridge. Oh and there's a no-fishing-from-the-bridge sign halfway across it."

"Somebody in authority has a sense of humor," Adam said. "Doesn't sound the least bit accommodating to my fear of heights, though."

"Nor my vertigo," Jolly added.

"If you're planning on taking in the view from the bridge, I suggest you gaze out over the entire expanse and not look down," she advised.

"Will do," Jolly said unconvincingly.

"I take it you two are not into mountain climbing," Carlita said.

"I once climbed Sugarloaf Mountain," Adam replied.

"Where's that?"

"Florida, not far from where I grew up. It's the highest point in the state—three hundred and twelve feet high to its summit."

"You conquered it by foot or car?" Carlita asked in jest.

"By bicycle. The twists and turns were harrowing."

"Three hundred and twelve feet up...my kind of mountain," Jolly said. I could jog that sucker."

"I didn't say how long or wide it was or you might rethink that statement," Adam said.

"Say fellas, does it appear to you Feldman is doing his share of swerving with that vehicle of his?" Carlita asked.

"I've noticed it," Adam said. "Every so often he hugs the shoulder of the road and then drifts over to the center line before straightening things out."

"It's New Year's morning. Maybe he and Daniela did a little too much celebrating at home," Jolly quipped.

"Like they did Christmas Eve," Carlita added.

Canon City came into view as US 50 began a descent into a valley. On entering the town, Jolly closed the distance with the Land Rover out of concern he might lose sight of it. "Well, here we are in the middle of prison valley," he said, bringing the truck to a momentary stop at an intersection.

The comment prompted a quizzical look from Adam.

"There are something like thirteen prisons in the Canon City area," Carlita quickly explained. "I'm not sure that includes the county jail," she added in jest.

"What's the population around here?" Adam asked. "Can't be much."

"County population is close to 35,000," Jolly said, keeping his eyes glued to the Land Rover. "The prison system has become an industry here. It includes both state and federal facilities. Prisoners are sent here from all over the place. Hell, you'll see more razor wire than barbed wire in these parts."

"The town's citizens must be paranoid living in this kind of environment," Adam said.

"From what I'm told, you see more uniformed guards walking around town than people in their civvies," Carlita said.

"It's not all gloom and doom here," Jolly said. "I understand many of the people who live off the prison system end up retiring here and liking it fine."

"The question is whether released prisoners end up retiring here?" Adam asked.

"No, they all go back to Denver," Jolly deadpanned.

"On the plus side, you have to admit it is a recession-proof industry," Adam said. "The economy goes down, crime goes up."

"Detective Jolly is personally responsible for a good chunk of the prison population here," Carlita said, tongue firmly in cheek.

"Maybe on the way back, we could find the time to stop, so you could visit some of your old acquaintances," Adam joshed.

"No thanks," the sheriff's detective said with certainty.

Once past the city, Jolly eased back to the previous interval with the Land Rover. Of growing concern, however, was the swaying back and forth of the target vehicle, which became more pronounced, raising concerns in the utility truck's cab.

"Something's wrong," Adam said, aware his companions were

feeling the same.

"Maybe it's the vehicle," Carlita suggested. "Could be he's in bad need of a wheel alignment."

They passed a power plant and a curio shop located at the corner of an intersecting road at which point US 50 resumed its climb up the slopes.

"How much further to the turnoff?" Jolly asked.

"Not far, if I recall right," Carlita said. "Feldman should be making his exit at any moment.

In the distance, the Land Rover could be seen making the turn.

"How far from the turnoff to the bridge?" Adam asked.

"Four or five miles," Carlita answered.

"What's the plan?" Adam asked straight out.

"What's the plan?" Jolly repeated.

"Yes. What do you have planned once we reach ground zero? It's but a short distance past the gorge."

"I figure we'll loiter a while at the bridge to give him enough time to get to the treasure ahead of us and start digging," Jolly said. "We need to catch him in the act to nail down our case."

The Land Rover was out of sight. "Not to worry," Jolly said. "We know where he's headed."

The county road leading to the gorge ended at the north entrance. From there the bridge was not yet visible, though the park attendant taking their fare assured them it was less than a mile away.

Crossing onto the bridge, they could feel the shudder of the span's wooden floor panels as they passed across them. Rising into view first were the towers of the bridge, held in place by suspension cables shimmering in the glare of the bright morning sun. They were followed in turn by the superstructure, a mass of galvanized wire bundled together to keep the bridge suspended above the gorge.

It was a majestic view, except for the fact it was interrupted by another spectacle—the sight of Feldman's Land Rover parked halfway down the narrow span.

"What the hell is he doing?" Jolly exclaimed, pulling the utility vehicle off to the side.

"He's in it, I hope," Carlita said.

"Fraley, there's a pair of binoculars in the glove department. Grab them and take a look," Jolly said.

Adam retrieved the binoculars and focused them on the Land Rover, close to two hundred feet away. "He's in there," he said.

"Do you suppose he's on to us?" Carlita asked.

Adam lowered the binoculars. "One way or the other, he's got to make a move. Time is not on his side."

Small groups of sightseers, undeterred by the biting wind, strolled up and down the bridge, occasionally daring to peek over the guard railing to the depths below.

Adam raised the binoculars for a second look at the Land Rover. The instant he did, the driver's side door flew open and Feldman stumbled out, a forlorn look wrapped across his face. Glancing about, he circled the back end of the vehicle in the direction of the bridge railing.

"What the hell!" Jolly shouted, as he and Adam hurled open the utility truck's doors and rushed down the wooden planks toward the suspect. Feldman had reached the railing and taken a sitting position on it facing the expanse below.

"Feldman—don't!" Jolly yelled on their approach. The suspect turned to face the two men and trailing woman closing in on him. On closer look, they could see his face looked drained and his shirt soaked in blood. He appeared disoriented, doubtlessly explaining his erratic driving. "Happy New Year, Jolly," he said and with no further ado launched himself off the railing and into the abyss.

Adam reached the railing first and peered down the deep, narrow fissure at the tumbling body until it finally disappeared into the harsh glare of the sun reflecting off the river. Talk about a scene-stealer, he thought, shielding his eyes from the glare to search in vain for where the body landed. He raised his vision and for a brief interim gazed out at the great expanse of landscape. A moment later, he again looked directly below, disregarding Carlita's advice, feeling at once the hypnotic and paralyzing sensation of a height foreign to his experience. Beauty and danger had combined into a mesmerizing lure. Abruptly, he took a step back.

"Did he jump?" a young child who had escaped from his parents' watch asked in earnest.

91

"Yeah, he jumped," Jolly said before the parents could scoot the child away.

Jolly also stood at the railing for a spell, braving the dizzying height to absorb the scene below before turning to address Carlita. "I'll call this in. Why don't you stick around and brief the emergency crews when they arrive. Fraley and I will head on over to the treasure site to see if it provides any sort of clues as to what's going on. We should be back shortly."

"You might want to take a look at this first," Carlita called over to them. While they were gazing into the abyss, she had slipped the keys from the Land Rover's ignition and opened wide the vehicle's trunk. Jolly and Adam stepped to her side to see what caught her attention. In full view was a vintage ornamental chest with its top sprung open. "Empty," she said, "but note the small clumps of dirt stuck to its sides, as if it's been recently exhumed."

"By whom is the question," Jolly said, eyeing the case carefully.

"Apparently not by Feldman," Adam said, "unless he did a late night run before your guy arrived for the stakeout. What time did they get it set up?"

"Not until early morning, shortly before he took off from the house. Apparently, someone called in sick, causing the delay. Nevertheless, there's no way he made two runs," Jolly said. "What I'd like to know is who put it there if not him and why?"

"The person or persons who have the gold put it there," Adam said. "It's a lame attempt to pile more suspicion on Feldman. They knew the cops would be tailing him and more than likely inspect his car at the appropriate time when the gold went undiscovered. The fact he threw them a curve also matters little to them. They've got the gold."

"He may not have known much of what was going on around him," Carlita said. "There's an empty liquor bottle in the vehicle."

Jolly phoned in the emergency and they were on their way.

"What do you make of it, detective?" Adam asked.

"I don't. All I have are questions. Was it because he lost the gold he took the leap or was it because he lost his wife? And what caused the blood? Could it have come from a self-inflicted wound, a failed suicide attempt that led him to take the surefire way out? Whatever, I just hope this isn't the end of it."

"End of it?" Adam asked, puzzled by the thought.

"Yes. Feldman, the perpetrator, ends his life and in so doing essentially ends the case. That's what the higher ups would want you to believe. Everything else, including the hoarding of gold and Daniela's role, is ephemeral and can be considered speculative."

Five miles west of the bridge appeared the unmarked road, barely distinguishable by the twin ruts carved out over time by mountaineers involved in unknown pursuits. Jolly followed the bobbing path for a mile across a landscape marked by thinned-out timberland, patches of snow and little else, until they passed a rise beyond which stood a grove of cottonwood trees standing naked in their stark black and white winter state. Spotting the trees, he pulled the utility truck off the road, steering it over hardened terrain to the perimeter of the stand. "Here we are," he said, engaging the brake.

Jolly retrieved the map from inside his jacket pocket the instant the two landed on their feet after hopping from the cab, a totally unnecessary move it turned out since less than fifteen yards from where they stood was a fresh carpet of dirt, approximately four by four feet in size.

"Well, we've learned one thing already. This isn't the end of the story," Adam said, approaching the patch. "Somebody does have the gold and it isn't Feldman."

Jolly dropped to a knee and ran his fingers back and forth across the freshly dug dirt where the hole had been. "See if you can find a small container of some kind in the truck," he said. "We need to take samples of this dirt back to make sure it matches up with what's stuck to the chest."

Adam checked the truck and returned with an empty litterbag.

Jolly grabbed several handfuls of the dirt and dumped them into the bag. "It's the same stuff, I'm sure," he said. He next stood and circled the patch, studying it closely. "They were careful not to leave footprints," he said.

"Interesting you say 'they,'" Adam said, taking his turn circling the area. "Let me ask you…does this look like the work of a person acting alone, a woman in particular?"

Jolly surveyed the scene a second time. "I take it you have Daniela in mind?"

"Looks like a hijacking to me and who better positioned to pull it off?"

"If so, she definitely didn't act alone," Jolly said. "Digging a hole, the size of a bear den, in ground this hard, calls for a strong back."

"Not to mention the lugging required to get the chest in and out."

"Let's get back to the bridge and touch base with Carlita," the sheriff's detective said, "and let's get rid of these damn things," he added, removing his hard hat.

* * * *

The emergency crews were still milling about when Jolly steered the utility truck back onto the bridge behind Feldman's abandoned Land Rover. There to greet them was Carlita. "What did you find out?" she asked, the anxiety in her eyes betraying the matter-of-factness in her voice.

"A hole in the ground that was no more, one large enough to stow the chest," Jolly said. "Get someone to check the chest for fingerprints," Jolly instructed her.

"The crime scene crew already did," she said. "It's clean."

"Which means Feldman likely didn't place it there," Adam said. "The people expecting it to be found are the ones who made sure it was clean of prints."

"Is the chest still in the trunk?" Jolly asked.

"Still there," Carlita said.

Jolly returned to the utility truck to retrieve the dirt samples he had taken. "Let's see if this stuff matches up."

Adam and Carlita followed him to the Land Rover and its opened trunk. Jolly shook a sampling of the dirt from the litterbag into one hand and broke off a clump from the chest in the other for comparison. He crumpled them separately in his palms and held them out for examination.

"Take a look," he said. "Same composition—same tiny small particles—same clay soil, for what it's worth. Carlita and Adam both looked at it and agreed. "Of course, it's the same soil found in most of

Colorado," the veteran detective said, seemingly undercutting his own argument.

Jolly dumped the samples onto the ground, patted his hands, and handed the litterbag containing the rest to Carlita for safekeeping. "We'll have the technicians take a look at it later." Shoving his hands into his pockets to ward off the cold, he looked in the direction of the bridge railing. "They retrieve the body yet?" he asked.

"They should have by now," Carlita said.

"How the hell did they get down there?" Adam asked, observing from afar.

"There's an incline train which takes you down and up," Carlita explained. "Do you want to take it down?" she asked.

"Are you recommending it?" Adam asked.

Carlita smiled. "Not this time of the year. You'll freeze your backside off. It's colder down there than up there. Plus, the railway adds to the coldness. It's nothing but a string of tight metal cages that haul you down at a forty-five-degree angle at three miles per hour. The winds whipping down the gorge add to the discomfort. Altogether, the ride is a five to six minute trip down, the same coming back up."

"What are the chances of it getting stuck?" Jolly asked. "I've been stuck on elevators and find it an uncomfortable experience to say the least, and those are indoors."

"They have safety measures in effect in case of a malfunction," Carlita said. "There are manually controlled stopping devices."

"You seem to know a lot of the specifics," Adam said.

"I should. I just returned from down there," she said. "I suggest you skip it and come back in the summertime, unless you enjoy watching chunks of ice float down the river instead of rafters. Like I said, things have been pretty much wrapped up down there, including the body. By the way, in case you're wondering, he hit the tracks, not the river."

"One is worse than the other?" Jolly asked.

"It is if you're riding the train and have to wait around for them to pick up the pieces," Carlita said. "By the way, I went ahead and notified Daniela. A news guy was nosing around and jotted down Feldman's license plate number before I had the chance to shoo him away. I thought it best she hear it from us rather than him."

"Her reaction?" Jolly asked.

Carlita rolled her eyes. "Not exactly a tearful one. She lashed out, claiming it was our hounding of him that drove him to his death."

"By chance, did the matter of the gold come up?" Adam asked.

"No, and I wasn't about to bring it up. She was in no mood to discuss details."

"Maybe she overcame the temptation to ask," Jolly said.

"Or else she already knew the details," Adam said.

"Carlita, why don't you hang around here for a while in case you're needed and then get one of the crime scene guys to give you a ride back? Fraley and I are going to head over to La Gulch Cantina to gather more info on the men in Daniela's life."

"Sure, but don't expect Daniela to be at work, if only for the sake of appearances," she said. "That may be the one temptation she can't resist today—wearing a smile on her face now that she's rid of him."

"All the better if she's not there," Jolly said.

CHAPTER ELEVEN

Owner Bob Chandler was on hand to greet them at La Gulch Cantina, escorting them to his office for the private interview Jolly had requested.

"You have a new partner?" Chandler asked, tilting his head in Adam's direction.

"A temporary replacement," the sheriff's detective said.

"You wished to speak with me about Daniela?" Chandler asked. "You do know she's not at work today due to the sudden death of her husband."

"Yes, we're aware," Jolly said. "We're also aware how inappropriate it may seem to be requesting an interview today but there are pressing circumstances regarding a major case we're investigating. Any delay could jeopardize the outcome."

"What is it you need to know?"

"Whatever you can tell us about her conduct, particularly anything recent that may have seemed out of the ordinary for her," Jolly said.

"Is she involved in a crime?" Chandler asked.

"That's what we're trying to determine," Jolly replied.

"Can you be more specific as to what sort of information? Is it personal or professional information you are after?"

"Let's start with the business side of her," Jolly said.

Chandler smoothed back the sides of his hair with the palms of his hands before coupling them in his lap. "Well, she's a good manager...keeps tuned in to the customers...shows up to work on time...firm with her subordinates...performance reviews are universally good. Altogether, I have no complaints with her work."

"And on the personal side?" Jolly asked.

"Again, can you be more specific?" Chandler asked, his dark brown eyes darting back and forth between his two visitors, though it was Jolly who up to this point had been firing all the questions at him.

"Did she have any inappropriate relationships with the staff or customers?" Jolly asked.

Chandler shook his head, clearly bewildered at the line of questioning.

The sheriff's detective was pushing the boundary of confidentiality, Adam reckoned. As with the car dealer, the owner's inclination was to cooperate, as long as the cooperation didn't come back to bite him in the butt.

Chandler shifted in his chair, gripped a crossed leg by the knee, and went for the disclaimer. "Can you assure me everything I have to say is off the record?" he asked.

"I can't guarantee you anything," Jolly responded, "though I can assure you all we're looking for at this time are leads to further the investigation."

Chandler gave a quick nod of the head and continued. "Danni...I call her Danni...is an ambitious, attractive woman. Nothing wrong with that combination in this business, or in any business I might add, especially if you're willing to use your attributes to further yourself as well as the business."

A lot of furthering on the table here, Adam mused.

"As for inappropriate relationships with staff or customers, I'll point out that if there were such instances they would have been reflected in her performance evaluations. Sure, there were rumors of questionable personal behavior, mostly spread by staff who felt Danni was demonstrating favoritism toward certain individuals. That's nothing out of the ordinary in the business world. Nor in the public sector, I'm sure," he added with a grin.

"Rumors of an improper behavior with anyone in particular?" Jolly asked. "A relationship other staff felt should be brought to your attention?"

Chandler uncrossed his leg and clasped his hands on his desk. "There was one occasion when the rumors rose to a level that required they be addressed. She and one of her subordinates, a server, were reportedly seen on numerous occasions going on breaks together, engaging in flirtatious banter, and they were even spotted out on the town after work hours. I spoke to her about the importance of maintaining a proper working relationship with her staff, especially subordinates, and that seemed to end it."

"This was recent?" Jolly asked.

"Yes, a month or so ago."

"Can you give me a description of the guy?"

"You want a description? I was expecting you to ask for a name."

"A description will do for now," Jolly said. "We have a profile in mind."

A guy who could do some heavily lifting, Adam thought.

"I'll do you one better," he said. "We keep photos of staff members on file."

Chandler strode to a file cabinet, fingered through some folders, and plucked out a photo. He handed it to Jolly who quickly scanned it before casually handing it over to Adam for his perusal. One of the huskier guys he recalled from his previous visit to the restaurant, a server who strutted the floor like a haughty matador. He handed the photo back to Chandler. "Does it fit your profile?" the owner asked of them.

"Close enough," Jolly said, raising a look of concern on Chandler's face. "What of her husband? What can you tell us about him and his relationship with her?"

Chandler hunched his shoulders. "He came across as obsessive in the contacts I had with him. He'd frequently call, wanting to know where his wife was or who she was with when told she was unable to come to the phone."

"Controlling," Jolly suggested.

"I wouldn't call it controlling. Danni is not a person to be controlled. She is the one who does the controlling. No, I'd say he was more concerned with losing her, knowing that he couldn't control her. He acted as if she was all he had left in life."

"You'd call it an obsessive love?" Jolly asked.

"More a possessive one maybe. However you define it, there was no question in my mind he was lost without her."

"Enough for him to take a leap off a bridge if he feared losing her?" Adam asked, jumping into the conversation.

Chandler flinched at the question. "Taking a leap for fear of losing her?"

Adam nodded.

The owner thought a moment. "Yes, I'd say it's within the realm of possibility. Is that what you think?"

"We're more interested in what you think at this time," Jolly said. "Is there anything else you can tell us about her background...like how was she able to land this job?"

"She had experience in the trade, in addition to having a college minor in hotel/motel management. Prior to coming here, she worked as an assistant manager at Barkers Lounge and Eatery. She interviewed well and..."

Mounted on the wall behind the owner's desk was a cluster of sports memorabilia, including a vintage wooden baseball bat. Chandler might as well have grabbed the bat off the wall and slammed it into Adam's stomach. "Barkers Lounge and Eatery," he repeated under his breath.

"...and received good references. It was an advancement for her, so she wasted no time accepting our job offer."

"How long did she work at Barkers?" Adam asked, no longer playing second banana in the conversation.

"Six months if I recall right."

"I think we may be getting off track here," Jolly said, unaware of the dramatic development churning in Adam's head.

That the sheriff's detective failed to make the connection came as no surprise to Adam. He had had virtually no time to check Reggie's place of employment. The interval between Jolly's locating the condo and the two of them showing up at his office was short, precluding a need for the detective to take the next step and check his employment.

Adam decided to hold his tongue on the matter. He needed to think things through before jumping to conclusions. He'd be the first to admit he was never a fast thinker. Give him time, however, and he'd become an accurate one. Put him in a think tank and he'd be okay. Put him on a debate team and there'd be no debate. The argument would pass him by.

"The guy you showed us the photo of…what's his name?" Adam asked.

"Carlos Ventura," the owner replied.

"Could we arrange an interview with him?" Adam asked.

"Sure. He'll be coming on duty in an hour if you want to hang around."

"Yes. I'd like to," Adam said, looking to Jolly for any objection. Instead, the detective thanked the owner for his cooperation and the two departed his office. "I'll call Carlita in to sit in on the interview with you. You're going to need a ride back to your car. I'd stay but I need to get back to the office to try and arrange another search warrant for Daniela's place," he said. "Somebody's going to grab that gold and make a run for it the first chance they have."

Adam moved to the public dining area and took a table with a view of the front entrance. He ordered a bowl of chips and salsa to nibble away the time. He had no appetite, much less answers to the questions eating at his stomach. He pondered the possibilities—or should they be termed coincidences? How coincidental was the link between Arlen Feldman, Daniela, and Reggie? Of minimal coincidence, he concluded, given the merry-go-round labor market of a restaurant trade located in an area of small to moderate size. Of greater coincidence was his ending up at Rita Feldman's cabin on Christmas Eve. That one he would like to chalk up to divine providence. Twas the season for it, was it not?

Carlita arrived first, spotting Adam's wave from where she stood at the entranceway. She has a nice gait, he noted on her approach, as graceful as her manner. "I was instructed to join you here," she said, sliding into a chair across from him. "Something to do with an interview, I was told."

"Yes. The guy we'll be interviewing is Carlos Ventura. He's a server here."

"What's his connection to the case?" she asked.

"He, like Daniela, also worked at Barkers Lounge and Eatery prior to coming here."

Carlita helped herself to a chip. "So?"

101

Beyond Carlita's shoulder Adam caught sight of Chandler at the front entrance conversing with Ventura. "The connection will become clear in the interview," he said, motioning with a bob of his head to the approaching matador.

"I understand you wanted to speak with me," Ventura said, helping himself to a chair next to Carlita.

"Yes. Did Mr. Chandler explain to you what this is about and that what you say to us is confidential?" Adam asked.

"He did."

"We were informed you worked at Barkers Lounge and Eatery before coming here, as did Daniela Feldman. Correct?"

"Correct."

"Did you have regular contact with Daniela during your employment at Barkers?"

"Yes. She was also my manager there."

"What would you say was her professional reputation among the staff there?" he asked.

Ventura flashed a wry grin. "Funny how I'm now in the position of doing the evaluating," he said, eliciting no smile from his inquisitor.

"Yeah, you never know when the tables are going to be turned on you," Adam said.

"Professionally, she was seen as effective and efficient," Ventura said, acting like he was relishing his opportunity to pass judgment on his boss. "She also was hardnosed at times."

"Was she fair in your opinion or did she play favorites?"

"She had her favorites," he answered with the slightest grin.

With you among them, Adam was tempted to say, but didn't.

"What about her personal side? Did she ever cross the line with the staff?" he asked.

The matador hesitated, like El Toro at the waving of the red cape. "When it was in her favor, she did," he replied, without asking what they meant by crossing the line.

Adam got to the point. "Did she ever have a personal relationship with one of the bartenders?"

"An affair?" Ventura asked.

Adam nodded.

"Is this relevant to the investigation?" he asked.

Adam figured by this time Carlita was asking the same question of him under her breath. "Yes, it directly relates to the investigation."

"It was no secret among the staff she was having an affair with one of the bartenders," Ventura replied.

"He was single?"

"Yes."

"Anything unusual about the pairing other than she was married?" Adam asked.

"Well, everyone was wondering why she picked that particular bartender to have an affair with. She was way above of his league when it came to physical attraction," he said, glancing at Carlita. "Plus, he was her subordinate. It wasn't like she was gaining any favor with the boss."

"Any idea why she decided to enter into the affair?"

"None whatsoever. He certainly wasn't a challenge for her. When Daniela goes into full flirt mode, she can have her pick of the pack."

Adam again was tempted to ask Carlos if he was among the pack. "Does Daniela have a temper?" he asked instead.

"Big time when not in public."

"What can you tell us about her husband?" Adam asked.

"Not much, other than he was always calling to check on her whereabouts."

"Did he ever show up at her workplace?"

"Never saw him there," he answered, following it with a chuckle. "Now that would have been one time she'd have put her temper on public display."

"Why's that?"

Ventura shrugged. "Just my opinion."

"Do you know the bartender she was having the fling with?" Adam asked.

"Knew him as a coworker, nothing more."

Perhaps feeling left out or tired of the two beating around the bush, Carlita asked the question she had no idea would strike at the heart of the investigation. "What was this guy's name, the bartender?"

"His name was Reggie Fielding," Ventura replied without hesitation.

Carlita cast a slow look Adam's way, inviting an explanation.

Adam ignored the invite. "That'll be all. Thank you for your input," he said to Ventura, excusing him from the table.

He returned his attention to the woman across the table who was staring at him with tilted head, still waiting for a reply to her invitation.

"Are you married?" Adam asked with a deadpanned face.

"Oh no, before we change the subject, please explain how long you've known your friend—"

"Acquaintance," Adam interjected, having already downgraded him.

"Okay, how long have you known your acquaintance was having an affair with the wife of our prime suspect?"

"I got wind of it this morning from our interview with the owner. He informed us Daniela previously worked at Barkers Lounge and Eatery. It came as a bolt out of the blue. That's why I wanted the interview with Ventura, to confirm there was a relationship."

"Did it come as a shock to Detective Jolly?"

"He was unaware Reggie worked at Barkers, so he didn't make the connection."

"You didn't tell him?"

"No. I wanted to talk to Reggie first to make sure if what we're hearing is true. On that point, Carlita, I'd like to keep it from Jolly until I have the chance to do so."

"Adam, I'm obligated to tell Detective Jolly everything I know about the case," she said determinedly.

"Can you hold off until the morning? You have my word I will tell him by then."

"If you don't, I will," she said.

"I understand."

"So you think Fielding and Daniela are somehow in this together?" she asked.

"Could be. Time will tell and the clock is ticking fast, for them and us. Jolly is right in saying a grab-and-go is imminent."

"Adam, I strongly urge you to avoid a confrontation with Reggie until Detective Jolly is brought up to speed."

"I agree, though I still have to face Reggie when I get back to his place."

"Like I said, a face-off is the last thing you want at this point."

"Have another chip," he said, nudging the serving bowl closer to her.

"Don't get me started on these or I'll have to add to my exercise regimen."

"You still haven't answered my question," he said.

"What question is that?"

"Are you married?"

Carlita furrowed her brow. "What's that have to do with anything we've been discussing?" she asked in return.

"It takes my mind off Reggie."

She smiled liked she carried herself, with disarming grace. "No, I'm not married."

"Are you a Colorado native?"

"No, I'm a native of Cuba. I came to this country as a part of the Mariel boat lift."

"So you spent time in my home state?"

"Yes, several years in Homestead before my family moved to Colorado."

"You prefer the mountains over the ocean?"

"Perhaps because of my experience on the boat lift, I enjoy streams and lakes, preferably bordered by trees, over large bodies of water. I like the shorelines to be within sight," she said. "Does that make any sense?"

"Makes perfect sense, considering your experience," he said. "What do you make of Detective Jolly?"

"He's old school. I don't need to explain to you what that entails, except to say I'm comfortable with it. My father was cut from the same cloth. He believed there was a right way and a wrong way to doing things, not another way, unless of course you could demonstrate without offending his sensibilities that the other way worked."

"Jolly came up through the ranks?"

"Yes. He started out as a foot soldier, handing out parking tickets and the like before moving up. I know he spent a good deal of time in the Cold Case Unit as a result of the impact DNA has had on the crime solving process. It gave the unit a big shot of adrenaline and shed the spotlight on a number of high profile cases. It also brought additional personnel and money into the unit. At one point, Detective Jolly was dividing his time between the Cold Case Unit and Missing Persons, another unit overburdened by the sheer number of cases. The latter, as you may know, is not a preferred assignment for most detectives."

"They're considered low priority cases, right?" Adam said.

"Some consider them low priority for the simple reason there is no crime for being missing, so they say. I don't agree with them. Sure, many of them are runaway cases that resolve themselves in a short period of time, but all it takes is for one of them to turn out to be a kidnapping and your tardiness in pursuing the case turns into a public relations disaster. Thank God that was not the case with Detective Jolly's daughter."

"One of his daughters went missing?"

"Yes, his older one, Sheila. His younger one's named Karen. Ironic, isn't it? The daughter of a Missing Persons Unit detective goes missing."

"What's the story?"

"Sheila was driving back from visiting a girlfriend across the state in Grand Junction at an odd hour of the morning and fell asleep at the wheel. Her car veered off the highway and over a small cliff. It ended up out of view, lodged sideways atop a grove of aspen trees. She was missing for four days."

"What were her injuries?"

"She broke her leg and collar bone, along with suffering minor bruises. In one way, she was fortunate in that the trees broke her fall. On the other hand, it was unfortunate in that the car could not be easily seen from above or below where it was lodged."

"I assume they searched along the entire route?" Adam asked.

"They did, but since there were no skid marks left on the road, there was no way they could determine if it was, in fact, an auto accident that caused her disappearance. There was the real possibility she could have been the victim of a random car hijacking or planned kidnapping. The media immediately began asking if she could be missing voluntarily. The questions they raised ran the gamut. Did she have a mental condition? Did she have a history of being missing? Was she having relationship problems? Was she having difficulties at work or school? They were asking the same questions the sheriff's investigators were asking of Jolly."

"So, how'd they end up locating her?"

"A couple of kids hiking through the hills decided to cross the highway at that specific spot and noticed the vehicle lodged in the trees. They notified the highway patrol."

"She was conscious when they found her?"

"Yes. She had brought along snacks, plus a couple of bottles of water that she rationed to keep her from going hungry. However, she was jammed into the car and had no way of getting out. She tried to flash the headlights and honk the horn but nothing was operable."

"Jolly must have been a basket case."

"He was, though he didn't show it. The story was all over the papers. Of course, there were those who assumed she was a runaway and claimed the department was devoting too many resources to the case, solely because she was the daughter of a detective on the force. It wasn't the case at all. All of the additional hours devoted to the search were performed on a voluntary basis," Carlita said pointedly. "By the way, on a much lighter note, are you aware Detective Jolly has a gold mining connection?"

"That so?"

"Last year his daughters talked him into entering the annual burro race up in Fairplay, Colorado. They thought it played into his streak of stubbornness."

"Where'd he get a burro?"

"His girls rented one for him as a birthday present."

"I have a problem conjuring up an image of Jolly riding a burro. His feet would be dragging the entire way."

"You don't ride them in the race. You lead them along by a guide rope. All the burrow carries is the traditional pack-mining gear from the gold rush days. The legend has it that once the prospectors struck gold there would be a race on their burros to see who could file the claim first."

"Did Jolly finish the race?"

"He finished, but at the end it was the burro leading him across the finish line. The photos his daughters brought back capture the moment. It was hilarious."

Carlita brushed aside a lock of hair from her forehead and raised another smile. "What about you? Did you rise through the ranks or is that an option in the private eye business?"

"There are only two ranks in my firm—office manager and owner. I started out as an office manager for Pete Peterson Private Investigations. When Pete retired to the Florida Keys several years ago, I took over the business. I renamed it Adam Fraley Private Investigations and hired a woman to fill the position I vacated."

"What's her name?"

"Tamra Fugit. Why?"

"Maybe it will become Tamra Fugit Private Investigations down the line," she said. "Is Tamra capable of filling your shoes?"

"More than capable."

"You must be a good mentor."

"I had the best mentor a fledgling investigator could have in Pete. I still seek him out for advice on occasions."

"Was it always your vocation to be a private investigator?" she asked.

"I wouldn't call it a vocation. It was more of a falling than a calling."

"You fell into the profession?"

"Yes. I needed a job to get me through college and that's how I ended up working for Pete."

"What was it you wanted to be growing up?"

"An explorer, but the big ticket items had all been scratched off the discovery list. The oceans, the continents, and the seas had all been taken. Outer space was the only thing left, but my interest in exploration did not extend beyond the earth."

"You know, Adam, when you boil it down, every profession requires exploration of some kind, including our own."

"That's exactly what I came to discover. We're all explorers when you come right down to it, with the ultimate goal of becoming a discoverer, whether it be an ocean or a swindler."

Carlita treated herself to another chip. "You should seek your former boss's advice on choosing vacation destinations. This one didn't turn out so well for you, did it?"

"It's not beyond recovery. I'll let you know when it's over if I need to take a makeup one."

"What's at the top of the list for your next trek?"

"All I know is it must be a spot where few others go."

"Name me a place," she said.

"Oh, I don't know...some remote hillside hamlet overlooking a quiet stream."

"You should become a travel writer and explore the world's unknown sites to your delight."

"Nice thought, but as I mentioned, there aren't many of those left," he said. "Tell me, if not a cop, what would you like to be?"

"A nun," she said straight out.

"You really are trying to take my mind off Reggie, aren't you?" he asked, waiting for the qualifiers or provisos to becoming a nun to start flowing.

"You asked me a question and I answered it," she said.

"Why?" he asked. "You'd be going from one end of the occupational spectrum to the other."

"It has to do with what you were saying, about going where few others go. The cloistered life has great attractions for the select few, solitude ranking high among them. Missionary work also appeals to me. I'm partial to people who work with their hands, the ones who are down in the muck, who immerse themselves in the conditions they are attempting to improve."

"Yet, you chose not to go that route," he said.

"I'm considering it as a second career," she said. "Did you know a growing percentage of those entering religious life are veterans of other walks of life—military and corporate retirees, widows and widowers among them. They often make the best novices or seminarians. You might keep that in mind, Adam, after you stop obsessing over Reggie."

Adam smiled at the notion. "Tough to do, Carlita."

"I do find one of the more difficult things in life is to determine your true friends," she said. "Sad to say, we often wear blinders in that regard."

"Agreed. My father was always saying it's the people you grew up with, the ones you can trace your roots to, who are the truest lifelong friends," he said.

"Another consequence of my family fleeing Cuba—leaving behind the friends I grew up with."

Adam pondered her for a moment. "So, tell me, what is your favorite recreation?"

"Favorite recreation?" she repeated.

"Yes. Say you had a day of leisure coming to you, how would you spend it?"

Carlita struck a thoughtful pose. "Well, if it was summertime, I would drive up to Boulder Creek not too far north of here, sit on my favorite rock near the waterfall, listen to the gurgling stream, and read a book."

Adam locked onto her clear green eyes. "Is there enough room for two on that boulder?"

"There is, and if it was summertime, or springtime, or fall, I'd ask you to join me," she said, a pleasant smile creasing her face.

"I'm going to consider that a raincheck," Adam said.

"You considered right."

A brief silence ensued between the two. "Come on, let me give you a ride to your car as Detective Jolly instructed me to do," Carlita said, breaking the silence. "It's been a long day already."

"And it's about to get longer," Adam responded.

Her parting words on dropping him off were to remind him of his responsibility not to jeopardize the case by keeping Jolly in the dark regarding Chandler's revelation or risking a confrontation with Reggie at this time. Sound advice, but in his view, there was no equivalency between the two. It was the issue of Reggie and their relationship that reigned uppermost in his mind.

* * * *

"What's up?" Reggie asked him on his return. "I wasn't sure I was going to see you before I head off to work. They have me marked in for a twelve-hour shift today. Have you had lunch?"

"No, it's been a busy day thus far. Haven't had time for much food."

"There's some snacks in the fridge in case you want to nibble," he said, throwing on his jacket. "Any developments in the Feldman case?"

Adam related the morning's events, including Feldman's death and the finding of the empty treasure chest, halting Reggie's trek to the door. "Wow! I'd say those are developments," he said, then paused for a moment, as if unsure of his follow-up question. "Any ideas on the whereabouts of the gold?"

"None."

Adam stepped a few paces to a compact bookshelf positioned above a television console stand. "Speaking of gold, I couldn't help but notice your book collection here," he said. Scanning the titles, he called some of them out, as Reggie looked on. "The California Gold Rush Experience, Sunken Spanish Galleons, Treasure of the Sierra Madre, Klondike Tales…"

"Yeah, I got interested in the subject while stationed in Florida. That whole Mel Fisher thing and his raising of the treasure ship the Atocha captured my fancy like everyone else's. It's been said one third of the world's mined gold still lies at the bottom of the oceans."

"Quite a collection," Adam said, pulling one book from the shelf and leafing through it.

"Do you realize the history of gold parallels the history of man?" Reggie said.

"That so?" Adam said, re-shelving the book he had in hand.

"It's true. From the Phoenicians to the pharaohs, to the Romans, to Solomon, to the Spanish explorers, to Montezuma, to all the gold rushes, it played a major role in the development of civilization, especially in its western expansion," he said, taking on the role of instructor. "One thing you won't find in those books, however, is who the first guy was to discover the stuff. No one knows that for certain. For all we know, it could have been some Neanderthal strolling along a creek bed and tripping over a rock with a vein of it exposed. Next thing you know he's showing it to another Neanderthal who's bowled over by the sight of it.

Before you know it—eureka! The first precious metal trade negotiations are under way." The topic appeared to have bred a new fervor in Reggie as he continued. "Yeah, that guy who discovered it didn't get his proper recognition. Come to think of it, you could make an argument his discovery tops all the other discoveries in its impact on the world."

"There's no arguing it was a great motivating force in history," Adam said, stepping away from the bookcase. "Didn't the gathering of foreign gold all come under the notion 'by right of conquest?'" he asked, offering Reggie a wane smile. "By right of conquest or by hook or crook," Reggie responded, offering a wry grin in return.

"Say Reggie, one more thing. While we were interviewing the owner of La Gorge Cantina, he mentioned Daniela once worked at Barkers Lounge and Eatery."

Reggie hesitated, his hand resting on the doorknob. He spun his frame halfway around to face Adam. There was a distant cast to his eyes, a hollowness in his words. "Really? She must have left before I came on board. I don't recall seeing her."

"How long have you worked at Barkers?"

"Less than a year," he said, swinging open the door before pausing again, as though to say something but didn't.

Adam realized he was engaging in a conversation in which the unspoken was of more consequence than the spoken, a sure indicator if there ever was one of a communication breakdown.

"Got to run. Don't forget the snacks in the fridge," Reggie said, continuing on his way out the door.

Adam mulled the situation over in the quiet of the early afternoon. Timelines raced through his mind, intersecting each other with disturbing frequency, jumbling his thoughts into a mass of confusion. He walked to the kitchen and snatched a phone book out of a drawer. He flipped through the yellow pages to restaurants and bars, settling his finger on an entry. Grabbing the receiver from a wall phone, he dialed Barkers Lounge and Eatery. "Yes, I'd like to speak to Daniela Feldman, please."

"Daniela no longer works here," the voice on the other end said.

"Oh, is that right. I'm an old acquaintance of hers travelling through town and thought I'd give her a ring. How long has she been gone?"

"Five or six months."

"Thanks. I'll try and catch her at home."

"An acquaintance of hers," Adam repeated to himself. Perhaps that best described his relationship with Reggie from the beginning, having served but a few months alongside him in the Air Force until life sent them on their separate paths. From friend to acquaintance was not a natural progression...or was he arbitrarily distancing himself for professional cover-your-butt reasons?

Adam again grabbed the phone and dialed his office manager in Tampa. He received no answer. He tried her at home, remembering it was New Year's Day.

"Watching the football games?" he asked on hearing her voice.

"A question I should be asking you, though obviously you're not," she said. "If you must know, I'm reading a book."

"Please don't tell me it's Treasure Island."

"I believe I'm beyond that level, Adam."

"I need your help," he said, more as a plea than a directive.

"Do I get double time for the holiday?"

"You get my everlasting gratitude."

"I'll be glad when your vacation is over so I can relax again. What is it you need?"

"Information on Reggie Fielding."

"The guy you're visiting?" she asked in surprise. "Here's a thought. Why don't you turn around and ask him whatever it is you need to know?"

"Can't," he said, without getting into the details. "Think of it as a background check. I may have mentioned to you at one time he was temporarily stationed at McGill Air Force Base where I got to know him. When his assignment ended, he returned to his permanent base here in Colorado. What I need to know is what kind of discharge he received and any other particulars you can dig up on him. A good place to start with is McGill."

"Adam, I hate to interject a sour note into the conversation, but McGill is not going to release personnel information to a private investigation firm."

Grasping at straws, was he? "Yeah, you're right," he said, sighing his agreement.

"Since you're back on good terms with the sheriff department's people out there, why don't you ask them to do the checking? The Air Force will listen to a law enforcement agency."

"You're right again, but I'm trying to avoid bringing the local officials into it at the present time."

"Didn't you once have a contact person in the sheriff's department here? Some guy your former boss was in good with?"

"I did, but he upped and left for a better position," he said, bringing the conversation to a momentary halt.

"Adam, there may be a way for me to access the military records after all," she said reluctantly.

"Nothing illegal, I trust," he said, his hopes tweaked.

"No, but requiring action above and beyond the call of duty, I might add. How soon do you need the information?"

"By this evening would be fine."

"Need I remind you, today is a holiday?"

"Air Force Security never takes a day off."

"Okay, I'll see what I can do," she said, resignation creeping into her voice.

CHAPTER TWELVE

Tamra drew a deep breath and dialed the sheriff's office. "Deputy Tommy Eanello, please."

"Hold on a moment. Let me see if he's on duty today," the man answering said.

If Eanello was off, Tamra ruminated while on hold, the good fortune would be hers. If not, it would be her boss's. "Deputy Eanello speaking."

She recognized the nasal toned voice right off. "Deputy Eanello, this is Tamra Fugit from over at Adam Fraley Private Investigations. The reason I'm calling is that I thought you might be able to help us on a case we are working on."

"Well, this is a great way to start off the New Year. What can I do for you, Tamra?"

She related in the most professional tone she could muster the information they were seeking.

"I don't see why we can't at least make the effort," he said. "We deal with base security all the time. They help us. We help them. How soon do you need the information?"

"As soon as possible, meaning today, I'm afraid. Otherwise, I wouldn't have bothered you on a holiday."

"No bother. Tell you what. It's three o'clock. I have a supper break scheduled at five. In between, I have a few chores to take care of. Why don't you meet me at Orologio's for an early dinner? By that time I should have something to report."

Tamra recalled the urgency in Adam's voice. It was time to take one for the team, she decided. "I'll be there at five," she said.

* * * *

A favorite hangout for the young, upwardly mobile, Orologio's had come down from its New Year's Eve high. Business was moderately brisk, but the buzz undoubtedly present the previous night had dissipated to scattered chatter.

It came as no surprise that Eanello was waiting for her inside. She had spotted a sheriff's car in the parking lot on her arrival. A hostess escorted them to a cramped corner booth at the deputy's suggestion. Past practice on his part, Tamra figured. She couldn't help but notice the deputy was carrying a small cloth bag, similar to a purse, sparking her curiosity. At the server's urging, they both chose the blackened chicken sandwich and red potatoes to dine on.

"Happy New Year," Eanello said, raising his water glass to her.

Tamra responded in kind, anxious for the small talk to pass quickly and painlessly.

"You're looking terrific," he said.

"Thank you."

"I'm curious," he said, leaning nearly halfway across the table. "What color lipstick is that you're wearing? Looks like there's a yellowish tint to the red. Almost matches the color of your hair."

"Close enough," she said, her eyes flashing a caution sign.

Eanello grinned. "Are you aware you have an edge to you?" he asked.

"One of the reasons I keep my distance from people. I don't want to cut them."

"I find it an attractive quality in a woman," he said, holding his grin.

Time to redirect the conversation back to idle chatter, she decided. "Tell me, what led you into law enforcement?" she asked, the question erasing his smirk.

"I decided to clear the family name for once and for all," he said, adopting a serious tone. "You know how it goes with Italians. The vowel at the end of the name is associated with crime no matter what."

"Tamra gave him an inquisitive look. "Not by me," she said. "There's Italian blood in my family."

"Okay, maybe not by you, but by a lot of others," he said. "I had a grandfather by the name of Johnny Eanello who was a notorious figure in these parts. He was known as the Robin Hood of South Florida. This was in the thirties during the prohibition period when everyone, especially my grandfather, was involved in some way or the other in bootlegging or illegal gambling. I can't tell you how many brushes with the law he had."

"I never considered Robin Hood as a notorious figure," Tamra said. "I always thought there was a good side to him, at least as he was portrayed in literature and films."

"From the public's perspective, there was a good side to my grandfather, mainly because of his involvement with bolita. He'd make a bundle of cash playing the game and then spread a good portion of his winnings among the poor in the community, including many of his relatives.

"What's bolita?" Tamra asked.

"It was a game popular in the Cuban and Italian communities. You go down to Ybor City and ask anyone about bolita and they will tell you all about it."

"Can't you tell me about it and save me the trip?" Tamra asked, her interest tweaked.

"It's very simple. It works something along the lines of a lottery. One hundred balls are placed in a container and jumbled thoroughly. Bets are taken on which ball will be drawn. Of course, there were many ways to cheat the system back then. Some balls were weighted with lead and ended up on the bottom of the container for easy pickings. Others would be placed in a freezer beforehand so they would feel cool to the touch."

"The game was illegal, you say?"

"It was illegal in Florida but bribes to the politicians kept it out in the open. Many people who never thought of themselves as anything but law abiding did not consider it a crime. After all, it wasn't that much different from the bingo being played in parish halls across the country. That was the general sentiment. My grandfather was a master manipulator of the game and managed to make his bundle while keeping one step ahead of the law. He knew he was engaged in illegal activity but didn't consider it sinful. Maybe that's why he spent as much time in the courtroom as he did church."

"You're portraying him as a saint and scoundrel at the same time," Tamra said. "To law enforcement officials I take it he was much more the scoundrel."

"He was as much a scoundrel to the cops as he was a saint to the people."

"What happened to him?"

"He was killed in a car accident. He was only in his thirties. He died broke, having given away all his money. He preferred doing that rather than saving it. He figured if he put it in a bank either the crooked bankers or the government would end up with it."

"And do you feel you've cleared your name?" Tamra asked, figuring it was not the case, considering the low profile position he held.

Eanello shook his head and grimaced. "To be honest I don't feel I was given the chance," he said. "I started off fine, to the point where I was hoping to make it to detective. I was getting excellent performance reviews, one right after the other. Things were definitely on the right track until they made me overseer of the evidence room. It was not long after, stuff started to disappear from the room and I came under suspicion."

"What sort of stuff?"

The deputy chuckled. "The evidence room is like a private shopping mall. It's contains everything imaginable—skateboards, bicycles, prescription painkillers, tools, cash, cameras, antiques of every kind. You name it, the evidence room's got it."

"Did you catch the thief?"

"Nah. It's too easy for the evidence technicians, the people who work under the overseer, to abscond with an item. Usually, they'll pick away at something, take a little cash at a time or snatch a portion of the drugs on hand. That way, it's not readily apparent something's missing."

"Aren't there checks and balances in place?" Tamra asked.

"Inventories are taken. Audits are conducted. Shelf lists are compiled. That still doesn't keep items from disappearing. You'd think in a law enforcement agency the evidence would be in safe hands. Yet, people are always wondering what the hell happened to their property when it's discovered it's missing. You can't blame them. Sometimes stuff doesn't even make it to the evidence room. I'm told in some of the large urban areas up north, detectives will drive around for a few days with the stuff in the trunk of their car before heading to a high crime area to sell it on the streets."

"Are these missing items you're referring to related to cases that are resolved or unresolved?"

"Both," the deputy replied. "There's always stuff that ends up unclaimed after a case is resolved. It can always be disposed of once the overseer signs off on it. It can be a complicated process. You're lucky you don't have to deal with an evidence room the size of ours."

"We don't even have an evidence room," Tamra pointed out.

Eanello reached to his side and lifted up the mysterious compact cloth bag he was carrying.

"You don't have a hundred bolita balls in there, do you?" Tamra asked half in jest while warily eyeing him.

The deputy reached into the bag and pulled out a small case, spiking the concern already building in Tamra's mind. He opened the case and retrieved from it a sparkling gold-plated woman's watch.

"Now, if you'll kindly hold your wrist out," he said.

Tamra's antenna was now picking up a strong signal. "No, I shouldn't," she said, hoping the server would hurry with the meals.

"Please, let me see how it looks on you," he urged, dangling the item in front of her.

Tamra relented against her better judgment and held her arm out over the table.

Eanello slipped the watch over her wrist and sat back to admire his work. "A perfect match," he said.

If there was anything she had learned in her relationships with men, it was not to let herself become beholden to them, especially to those with whom she had no interest in building a relationship in the first place.

"This isn't by chance an item from the evidence room, is it?" she asked, her arm still extended.

"By chance, it could be," he said, a wide devilish grin forming on his narrow face. "Items that are never reclaimed following the resolution of a case sometimes get lost in the shuffle or are inadvertently dropped from the rolls."

Tamra withdrew her arm. Visions of a front-page photograph showing her wearing a key piece of evidence in an imaginary homicide case burst into her consciousness. She glanced about for a mounted security camera. Instead, her eyes were drawn to a young couple occupying an adjacent booth looking their way, doubtlessly wondering if some romantic gesture was being consummated. She quickly slipped the watch from her wrist and handed it back to the deputy. "Please return it to wherever it came from," she said forthrightly.

Eanello shrugged, took the watch in hand, and placed it back into the case from whence it came.

She realized she was risking his reneging on the Reginald Fielding information but the end justifying the means only worked with her when applied within the parameters of the law.

Eanello leaned back and slipped a small notebook from his shirt pocket. "Okay, down to business," he said, flipping it open. "Here's what I found out about your Reginald Fielding. His service record was pretty much clean through his temporary assignment at McGill. It's when he returned to his permanent station in Colorado that things started to turn sour for him. The record shows he ended up receiving what is called an 'Other than Honorable Discharge.'"

"Where does that rank among the less favorable discharges?" Tamra asked.

"It's more serious than a general discharge and less serious than a dishonorable one. It's an administrative action requiring no court martial. Basically, they kick you out for bad behavior."

"His bad behavior was...?"

"Inappropriate advances to an officer's daughter—not once, mind you, but twice. According to the official narrative, he received a stern warning after the first incident and ignored it. The second got him booted."

The server brought their meals. Anxious to get the news to Adam, Tamra at once dug in, attempting to hurry through hers without appearing rude.

"Is it fair for me to ask if we can do this again?" the deputy asked, finishing off his last bite.

"It's fair, but if it's a date you have in mind, I'll have to pass," she replied in her best diplomatic manner.

"Are you seeing someone?"

"Yes," she fibbed, opting for the literal interpretation of the question.

"I knew it," he said, as if the revelation relieved the earlier putdown of him. "Let me guess, it's your boss."

Tamra hesitated. "Good guess," she said, playing hard to pin down, knowing there might be a hidden desire buried in her response somewhere.

"If it's not your boss and he's free and single, he's in bad need of an eye exam."

Duty completed, Tamra rushed home and was on the phone to Colorado to relate her findings to her boss. "This may not come as good news to you, Adam," she said in conclusion, "but I trust something good will come from it."

"The truth always leads to goods things," he said in response, as though offering up a platitude.

"Adam, come home soon," she said, her tone spontaneously shifting from the professional to the personal.

"Believe me, home is looking better by the minute, Tamra."

* * * *

Alone with his thoughts, Adam sat in the darkness of Reggie's living room, resting his eyes as he pondered recent developments. In the background, the sounds of John Denver wafted in from a nearby condo. Incongruous, he thought, listening to John Denver in the dark of night as opposed to the dawn of day, preferably on a mountaintop. Not unlike listening to Jimmy Buffet in the early morning instead of on a sultry Florida summer afternoon while lying by the pool. Perhaps in the same vein, he was seeing Reggie in a whole new light.

What did the timeline of events tell him? For one thing, Reggie knew of Daniela before he, Adam, had even set foot in Colorado. It was a knowledge Reggie gained not from professional acquaintances or newspaper accounts, but from personal association, something he had failed to inform Adam the day he was digging up information on Arlen Feldman's background. Why didn't Reggie let him know at the first mention of Daniela's name that he knew of her? Because stuff, romantic or otherwise, was already going on between the two behind the scenes, Adam now realized. The fact Feldman had socked away his haul in some mysterious manner was not lost on them either. Why not wait and see where the sheriff's investigation and their own led? Somewhere along the line, the secret to where the loot ended up would be unearthed, and courtesy of Adam and his hypothesizing, it was. No, it did not necessarily follow that Reggie was directly involved in Rita Feldman's death, though it could not be completely ruled out at this stage. Certainly, there was nothing out of the ordinary in their crossing of paths. As posited, the restaurant business was a mobile profession. Workers bounced from one eatery to the other, picking up friends and acquaintances along the way, not to mention the occasional lover. Still, save for the Other Than Honorable Discharge, everything else was conjecture. In the morning he would have to face his host, the man whose food he was eating, whose guest bed he was sleeping in, whose military life he had shared, if only for an interim.

John Denver faded, as did Adam into a troubled sleep for which there was no remedy, excepting the possibility it was all one big misunderstanding on his part.

CHAPTER THIRTEEN

Adam awoke with a start, his inner alarm shouting it was time to get up, for what reason he was unsure. That was until he realized like a homeowner returning to his burgled house that something was missing. He sat on the side of the bed, flipped on a desk lamp, and glanced at the clock aside it. Five-thirty in the morning. Gathering his senses, he sauntered from his bedroom to the sliding glass door leading to the outer deck. An overnight cold front had left a ring of frost along the edges of the glass pane. Sliding the door open, he stepped outside into the chilled air in his t-shirt, shorts, and bare feet. He leaned over a railing to survey the parking lot below. Reggie's slot was empty. He stepped back inside and checked the master bedroom. He found the bed undisturbed. The missing something was Reggie. On a hunch, he checked the storage closet. Along with Reggie, the footlocker was missing. He returned to his room and threw on some clothes before hustling back to the living room. The lid had come off the boiling kettle, letting escape all pretense. The show was going on the road with two of its leading players now on the lam.

He plucked from Reggie's desk a Colorado road map he had referenced prior to his trek to Canon City with Jolly and Carlita. One question was uppermost in his mind. What was their likely escape route? To be sure, they had to travel fast and far to evade the encirclement certain to descend on them once the authorities moved into action. No better way than by air, he calculated, recalling Jolly's revelation that Daniela possessed a private pilot's license.

He opened the map and scanned it for airport locations—nearby ones, small ones, out of the way ones—where suspects on the run could slip away with little notice and by the next day be half a continent away. By impulse it became a last-in, first-out exercise for him, for sitting in the front of his mind was the image of a signpost at a Highway 50 intersection near Canon City alerting travelers to a county airport a few miles up the road. He remembered thinking at the time what a convenience for those eschewing the climb up the slopes by car.

Tracing the in points of the map with his finger, Adam located the airport. If nothing else, it met the quick getaway criteria but so did others. Sliding his finger from the airport symbol he had landed on, a feature of another sort caught his attention. Was that a faint pencil checkmark near the airport symbol? He raised the map closer to the light to examine the mark. Yes, it was a partially erased checkmark. He opened the desk drawer and spotted a loose pencil among the myriad items. With it, he placed another faint checkmark adjacent to the original one. The same shade of lead, he noted. He sat back, rubbed his temples, and considered the possibilities. If this was the airport the suspects chose, their options were limited when it came to pre-flight preparations. No doubt, the operating hours of an airport of this size and location were restricted to the daylight period. Anyone planning a quick getaway would like to be positioned close by when it opened. He grabbed the phone book and found the listing for the airport. He dialed the number and promptly received a recorded message informing him the facility opened at eight in the morning.

Taking a quick tally of events, Adam strolled to the outer deck's glass doorway to glimpse the breaking dawn. The rising sun had lit the tips of the towering mountain summits. Reggie was not at home nor was Daniela, he was convinced, though the latter he decided to verify. He returned to the desk and checked the phone book. As expected, the Arlen Feldman residence was among the listings. He dialed the number and again received a recorded message informing him the residents were unavailable at the moment to come to the phone and could the caller please leave a message. The voice on the recording was unmistakably Daniela's.

Adam redirected his attention to the map. The whereabouts of Reggie and Daniela was now the issue. A cold front had muscled its way down from the mountains, dropping temperatures below freezing. If the two were planning on sitting in a parked car for hours on end outside the airport entrance, it was one exposure they could do without. Once more, Adam checked the phone book, this time for lodging approximate to the airport. He jotted down the numbers for the only two within getaway range—the Treetop Lodge and the Crestview Inn. He dialed the Crestview first, getting on the other end of the line a man with enough gravel in his voice to fill a quarry.

"Yes, this is an emergency call," Adam said, summoning up his most authoritative voice. "It concerns a death in the family. We are trying to locate the next of kin and have reason to believe they may be staying in your inn. Their names are Daniela Feldman and Reginald Fielding."

"Hold on," the man said.

Adam measured with the pencil he had in hand the distance from each of the motels to the airport. They turned out to be equally distant, though located in opposite directions of the facility.

"There are no registrations under either of those names," the man said with finality.

"Is there anyone listed under the last name Diaz?" he asked, testing the guy's patience.

"Hold on," the man said in frustration.

The notion of it all being a big misunderstanding crept back into Adam's consciousness. He found himself wishing it was so.

"No Diaz either," came the clipped response.

He rang the Treetop Lodge and was greeted by a young woman as cordial as the previous clerk was coarse. He repeated his emergency line and the two names he was after. Moments later, she was back on the line. "I'm sorry, sir, but there is no Feldman nor Fielding registered here."

"Do you have a Daniela Diaz listed?"

"One moment please."

Adam restlessly tapped the pencil on the desk as he contemplated his next move, if such existed.

"There is no Daniela Diaz," the clerk informed him. "However, there is a Danni with an 'I' Diaz registered."

"Danni Diaz?" Adam said.

"Yes, do you want me to ring her?"

"No, that's not necessary," he said. "I need to check something else first. Thank you very much."

Adam immediately dialed the sheriff's office and requested the home number of Vernon Jolly. When told it was against department policy to provide such, he requested that the department contact Jolly at home and have him call Adam Fraley. It had to do with a major case the sheriff's detective was working on. As he sat and waited, he debated whether to take matters into his own hands and head for the mountains, an option he was about to embrace when the phone rang.

"This better be good, Fraley."

Adam related the overnight developments, underscoring the urgency to act without simultaneously sounding overbearing.

"Meet me at the same truck stop off the interstate we met before," Jolly said.

* * * *

Jolly had jettisoned the utility truck in favor of an unmarked car.

"Where's Carlita?" Adam asked, hopping into the vehicle.

"She's on her way to the Feldman residence to check it out. The search warrant has been issued."

Jolly steered the car onto the interstate. It was an hour's drive to the Treetop Lodge, much of it over the same route they had taken to the Royal Gorge. Barring unforeseen circumstances, they should make it in time.

"So why was it at our meeting with Chandler you elected not to tell me of the connection between Daniela and Fielding?" Jolly asked, settling the car into cruising speed.

"I wasn't sure at the time there was a connection. Restaurant workers are always jumping from one eating establishment to the other. I needed to verify there was overlap in their employment at Barkers and there was. There's no question they knew each other."

"Which means she knew exactly who it was you were with in the parking lot tape," Jolly said. "But does it follow they were co-conspirators?"

"The fact he kept it hidden is proof enough for me there was something going on between the two," Adam said. "That, plus the look on his face when he denied having worked with her."

"How long have you known this guy?"

"He was on temporary duty at the same air base I was stationed at. We hung around a bit like guys assigned to the same unit often do. I wouldn't classify him as a bosom buddy, more a former buddy. After he returned here from Florida, we kept in contact."

The police radio crackled in the background as the dispatcher relayed calls in staccato style.

"He was in good standing with the military?"

"Until he neared the end of his four-year stint, yes. He had to be, working in a base security unit."

"Any idea why he went to the dark side?"

"In the Air Force instance, it simply could have been a case of misplaced affection. Reggie seems to have had little success with the ladies. He's also been facing some financial difficulties, though they're not insurmountable by any means. He was keeping a few paces ahead of the creditors, as far as I could tell. In the Feldman case, I believe it was the combination of a willing woman, a chest full of gold, and a private plane ready to whisk them both out of the country that got the best of him. Now that I look back on it, the Other Than Honorable Discharge could have impacted his job prospects. Running your own security firm, as he did for a while, is one thing. Working for someone else is another. You don't have to worry about passing a background check when it's your operation."

"'Lead us not into temptation' is not a tactical consideration of law enforcement," Jolly said. "Several years ago we had a fellow on the force who was working the prostitution beat. He was a good family man—nice wife and three kids. Unfortunately, he ended up falling hard for one of the hookers."

"How long had he been on the force?" Adam asked.

"Fifteen years and he had a solid record for every one of them. However, it didn't help him from falling victim to what I call the unholy trinity of temptation: money, drugs, and sex."

"Did they run him through any kind of rehab process?" Adam asked.

"They tried heavy-duty counseling, but he was in too deep with her for it to do any good. It was equivalent to telling a schizophrenic of long standing to snap out of it."

"I take it the marriage didn't survive," Adam said.

"The marriage didn't survive nor did his career on the force."

"What about his relationship with the hooker?"

"It's the old story. The steam went out of it the moment his wife left him. Last I heard she was still working the streets."

"And the undercover guy—where'd he end up?"

"I have no idea, nor do I care. He made his own bed and decided to sleep in another. Look what it got him."

"Did you know Shakespeare willed his second best bed to his wife of many years?"

"Meaning what?" Jolly asked. "Was he taking a little jab at her from the grave?"

"Everybody was making a big thing out of it when it was revealed, claiming it was evidence of how he really felt about her," Adam said. "However, wiser heads pointed out that in Elizabethan times, the best bed was always saved for guests. The second best was the marriage bed."

"Glad they got that straightened out," Jolly said. "I'd hate for old Will to go down in history as a cad."

"It also says something about evidence, don't you think?"

"Like what?" Jolly asked.

"Like much of what you see is outward appearance. What lies below or beyond it often holds the real meaning."

Jolly doused the vehicle's lights. The sun had risen, spreading sheen across the landscape. In the distance, the mountains stood tall, their fresh winter coats on full display.

"Your gold-hoarding idea…"

"You don't need to say it," Adam interjected. "It's what set events in motion. Reggie tipped off Daniela as to what was occurring with the investigation and the two conspired to separate her husband from the gold. As soon as she left the interview with you, I'm sure she contacted Reggie."

"The question is, did she know of the stash and where it was hidden all along," Jolly said.

"She either learned of it at the interview or somehow wiggled it out of him earlier in their relationship."

"The somehow could have been a threat from her to implicate him in his ex-wife's murder by denying him his alibi of being home at the time of her death," Jolly said. "By the way, Fielding and Daniela would have known each other at the time of Rita's murder, according to your timeline. Who's to say Reggie didn't have a hand in it?"

The notion sent a chill through Adam. "Reggie may be a sucker for a pretty face, but I have a tough time picturing him as a killer. If you recall, it was Feldman's car I saw that night. I doubt he lent it to Reggie. No, he didn't jump full board into it with Daniela until my hoarding theory was thrown out there."

"So, you're not convinced Daniela rushed home after the interview and confronted her husband on the spot."

"If she did, she was accompanied by Reggie, which could have set up a spontaneous combustion situation, particularly if her husband suspected her of having an affair all along. Why else would he have ended up getting bloodied?"

"On that note, the medical examiner reported it was a knife wound. "Not deep, nor fatal," he said.

"What time did the stakeout get set up?" Adam asked.

"Not until early the next day, sometime around six in the morning. The assumption was he wouldn't go looking for the gold before daylight. The irony is the assumption was both right and wrong. He may have originally intended to check on it but ended up carrying out a death wish as a result of a confrontation. It could be he passed out from the loss of blood and woke up in the morning to find out his world had fallen apart."

"I'm correct in saying Daniela's car was parked at the house during the stakeout?" Adam asked.

"Yes. Hers alone."

"Why did he let them get away with it? Why not notify the cops?" Adam wondered aloud.

"As you said, his world had come crashing down. Strange as it may seem, he could have still been in love with her. No question their relationship was a volatile one. It appears they were two of a kind in the temperament department. For all we know, it may have been what sparked their interest in each other. As for why he didn't contact the cops, the answer is simple. He hated us for all the trials he perceived us as having put him through. Why then give us the satisfaction of implicating himself in the fraud case as well as the murder?"

"What puzzles me is why they placed the empty chest in Arlen Feldman's car," Adam said.

"A diversion to gain time by muddying the waters is my guess," Jolly said. They figured we'd eventually discover it and get sidetracked when we realized he wasn't going for the gold."

"Pretty risky for them to count on us discovering it."

"What's the downside? They already had the gold and were on their way," Jolly pointed out. "No, not a particularly brilliant move, but then you don't put a lot of thought into things when your instinct is to grab the prize and run. They weren't sticking around for anybody's funeral, that's for sure."

CHAPTER FOURTEEN

Carlita stood in the pathway leading to the Feldman home. There was much to admire of the small townhouse tucked among the evergreens in the Colorado foothills, a favorite place for architects, writers, painters, and photographers, not to mention the occasional criminal, to put down stakes.

Daniela and Arlen Feldman were clearly fond of stone architecture and landscaping. The home featured a rock veneer exterior and a wide shingle roof overhang. A pebble pathway, bordered by stone retaining walls covered with clusters of shrubs led to the front entranceway. A gravel driveway completed the rugged look.

Inside the house, two deputies were executing a no-knock search warrant, though the no-knock part of it was not needed. The door was left unlocked. Why lock it when you don't plan to return, Carlita mused. She was handling the exterior search. There were two items of particular interest on their search list: the gold and the knife. The medical examiner's report stated Arlen Feldman had received a stab wound, probably from a small knife. However, it was not the cause of death. It was the fall that killed him.

Carlita walked up the gravel driveway to where Reggie Fielding's jeep was parked, leading her to conclude the two were on the run in Daniela's Chevy. The car was unlocked and the keys were in the ignition, another indication the two were in full flight and unconcerned with what they left behind. Nothing in the front seat area, including the glove compartment, gave her pause, except that the gas tank registered close to empty when she ignited the engine. The backseat area was another story. Sprinkled across the upholstery were tiny lumps of dirt, similar to the dirt found on the treasure chest in Arlen Feldman's vehicle. How they had transported the chest back to the house was no longer a mystery.

She began to scour the surrounding grounds, starting with the gravel driveway. She had scarcely moved a step from the jeep when a glint from the ground caught her eye. An object in the shape of a coin was interred among the gravel stones and casting off a yellow hue. She stooped to examine it. Taking it in hand, she retrieved a penny coin from her pocket and scratched it across the surface of the stone. She looked for a yellow mark on the penny. There was none. She could do what the old prospectors did and bite into the stone to test if it was malleable but she wasn't a prospector, at least in the traditional sense. She instead slipped a pen from her shirt pocket and pressed it hard into the stone's surface, discovering she was unable to make a dent in it. In a final act, she held the rock up to the sunlight, deciding it was more of a bronze than a canary yellow. Though a geologist she was not, she decided what she was seeing was not the precious metal. She dropped the stone back onto the driveway and in so doing, discovered her little fool's gold experience was not for naught. From her stooped position, she noticed several stones a few feet away with what appeared to be tiny red stains covering them. She donned her gloves and examined them closely under the bright morning sun. Confident they were bloodstains, she stood and surveyed the immediate area. She discovered a cluster of several more stones with the same red markings nearer the carport.

Carlita stepped back to visualize the scene as it might have appeared the day of the knifing incident with Arlen Feldman's Land rover and Daniela's Chevy parked in the carport and Fielding's jeep stationed behind them on the driveway. She posited the sequence of events. Either Daniela knew all along where the gold was hidden or she'd learned from the interview with Detective Jolly of its existence. Once she left the meeting, she immediately went into action, contacting Fielding to let him know the situation, whereupon they made a dash to retrieve the chest, transferring the gold to another container and placing it in Daniela's Chevy. But why the confrontation? That was the big question. Would her husband not have been pleased she beat the cops to the punch? Or more likely, was he unaware of her relationship with Fielding and became enraged when it dawned on him his wife and Fielding were about to make a run for it, leaving him behind empty-handed, of both his wife and gold?

Carlita gathered all the bloodstained stones and placed them in an evidence bag. She then proceeded to search the entire exterior grounds. As she did, the two deputies who were searching the interior of the home returned outside. They reported bloodstains on the floor leading to the kitchen and stains in the kitchen. They did not find the weapon nor did they uncover any gold. On hearing this, she instructed them to notify the lab team to come out and take a look at the stains.

Having examined the grounds, Carlita looked beyond the Feldman property to a neighboring estate partially hidden by the evergreens. She decided a visit to the neighbors would be in order. Traipsing through the trees, she came upon a structure not unlike the Feldman abode, save for the landscape, which was far less rock and more shrubs. She knocked on the door and was greeted by a slender, almost frail-looking man, with waves of white hair and bearded face. "Yes, ma'am. What can I do for you?" he asked in an engaging manner.

Carlita identified herself and the reason for the visit. "We're investigating an incident that occurred at your neighbor's house across the way," she said with a tilt of the head.

"Okay," he said, drawing the word out to signal his inquisitiveness.

"We believe it happened either New Year's Eve or early New Year's Day. Can you tell me if you heard anything unusual during those time periods?"

"I don't know if you'd call it unusual but I heard raised voices coming from that direction very early New Year's Day. I thought at the time it was nothing more than a New Year's Eve party that was still not ended."

"What time was that?" she asked.

"Had to be around five in the morning. I'm an early-to-bed, early-to-rise guy, so it wasn't too far in advance of me getting out of bed."

Carlita adjusted her posited timeframe. So, it was in the morning and not the previous evening the incident occurred.

"How many voices did you hear?" she asked.

"Difficult to say. Three or four at the most."

"Male and female?"

"Yes. One or two males and a single female, it sounded like."

"They were shouting at each other?"

"I hope it wasn't at me," he said, patting his chest.

"Would you describe them as heated words, like they were arguing?"

"At first, I thought they were celebrating, but it quickly became apparent, it was something along the lines of what you describe."

"You didn't get the gist of the argument?"

"No, I really wasn't paying that much attention to what they were saying. The whole episode blew over quickly. If it had dragged on longer, I would have called you people."

"Is there anyone else living here who might have heard the incident?"

"My wife was here, but she slept right through it."

"Do you know the couple that lives there?"

"Know them well enough to say hello. That's about it."

"Did you spend Christmas Eve at home also?"

The man smiled through his beard. "I was already asked that by the police. I was away with my wife visiting relatives."

Carlita thanked the man and headed back to the Feldman property. On departing the premises, she noticed through the tiers of pine trees lining the ascending slopes another neighboring estate situated on a clearing high above the Feldman residence. Pondering whether it was worth the effort to make a visit, she opted to take the hike up, more out of a desire for some outdoor exercise than an overriding sense a case-closing clue awaited her there.

Carlita set off through the woods, breathing deep the lung-cleansing mountain air. She passed through the first pickets of snow-capped trees into a narrow stretch of open land through which ran a dirt pathway. She followed the path for a short distance, noting a 'Deer Trail' marker posted beside it to alert hikers and bikers to the potential presence of the animal. City dweller that she was, it had been a while since she had seen a deer but the way she was crunching snow beneath her boots, the likelihood of her spotting one on this occasion was remote. She turned from the open pathway back onto the wooded incline, taking a more direct route through the trees to the home on the hill. Several paces into the woods, her gaze drew to a round mound of something other than timber and snow. She edged toward the object lying near a large pine tree a short twenty feet away. The moment the branched horns came into view, she recognized it for what it was: a deer carcass, and a half-eaten one at that. Not her preferred way of seeing a deer, she ruminated. She edged closer to the remains. It was a fresh kill and not by human hand, an act of raw ferocity that froze her in her tracks. A deathly quiet settled on the scene, broken abruptly by a sharp hiss, loud enough to scatter a flock of crows from a nearby tree. Carlita needn't look above her to figure out what lurked there. The circle of paw prints surrounding the kill was all the verification she needed. She slowly took a step back. In the same instant came the stir of tree limbs, as the cat slid from his perch onto the ground, bringing along with him a cascade of snow. A large male mountain lion landed in a crouched position next to his kill. His close-set amber eyes bore directly in on Carlita. In one simultaneous move, he bared his impressive incisors made more impressive by a ring of blood circling his mouth, pinned his ears back to announce to the trespasser whose territory this was, and let out a snarl that flushed more birds.

Carlita eased her hand over her holster while striving mightily to stay calm. The checklist of what to do when confronted by a mountain lion raced through her mind. "Okay, will do," she said to herself. She would avoid sudden movements, back away slowly while facing the animal, try to appear larger than she actually was, and talk firmly to the cat. The last one she decided to forego. This was one male that was definitely in no mood to listen to female chatter.

She took a second step back, prompting another chilling snarl from the cat. Unnerved as she was, her last desire was to shoot him. The cat was gorgeous; she would be the first to admit. His tawny coat was blemish free and his frame and face in perfect proportion. His recent behavioral pattern was another matter, though what he was up to at the moment was strictly according to the laws of nature.

In a single slow movement, Carlita lifted her revolver from its holster and raised her arms high in the best ogre stance she could summon up. At once, the cat lowered its crouch position, as though to pounce. Her predicament now was a straightforward one. She could shoot the animal in its stationary position or continue her slow retreat and in so doing, risk a much tougher shot if the cat did attack. Whoever said you never feel as much alive as you do when facing imminent death had it correct, she came to realize in the heat of the moment.

She continued her mime-like backward movement, increasing steadily the distance between her and the predator. Suddenly, as if it lost interest, the mountain lion relaxed from its crouched position, turned to snatch the deer carcass with his formidable teeth, and began dragging it closer to the tree, perhaps to cart it up with him this time around. Whatever, she wasn't waiting around to find out, quickening her retreat until the cat disappeared from view by the lines of pine trees. Still, she back-stepped down the entire slope before resuming her normal gait and holstering her revolver.

The fellas aren't going to believe this one, she reckoned. Now, if she was covered from head to foot with scratches and bite marks, they might buy into it. The further removed she became from the site of the encounter, the less inclined she was to share her experience. Maybe ten years down the line, when tall tales were being bandied about over a drink, she would offer hers up. In the meantime, she would classify it as nothing more than a random siting. As for the house up on the hill, she decided it was too distant for its occupants to have overheard anything beyond what the neighbor she had just interviewed heard. The mountain lion had no influence on her decision, of course, she tried to convince herself. On second thought, maybe it did.

Focusing her mind back on the case, Carlita was able to amend her scenario a bit with the help of the neighbor's input. Daniela and Fielding arrived home in advance of the stakeout man coming on duty, which meant they were on the road to and from the burial site in the wee hours of the morning. Daniela unquestionably knew exactly where the gold was buried. Whether her husband went along for the ride to the site was an open question. Doubtful, she reasoned, with Daniela or Fielding running the show. No, what was entirely possible was Daniella telling her husband she would be working until the early hours of the morning, given it was New Year's Eve. She then could have hooked up with Fielding for the dash to the burial location, which raised another question. The Royal Gorge Bridge would not have been open those hours of the morning. They would have had to loop around to the southern approach to the bridge rather than the normal northern one to reach the target site. If they left around one-thirty or so in the morning, that would have given them time to make the round-trip run. But why the round trip? Why didn't they just drive off with the stash once it was in their possession? she asked herself. Detective Jolly had the answer to that, she recalled, when he phoned her earlier in the day to let her know he and Adam were on the road to the airport. "They have a far better chance by air," he said. "Traveling the open road, they have little chance of escaping the widening net. The fact is the freedom of the road no longer applies to them." As to why they didn't just pick up and fly off, he pointed out the need for them to have at least a day or two of pre-flight preparation.

Carlita took one last look around the Feldman property. Eyeing Fielding's jeep, she hit on one final point. The drive to the Royal Gorge and back was no short jaunt, particularly when you had to take the long route around due to the bridge being closed. Filling the gas tank prior to undertaking the journey was simple common sense. She had noticed a filling station on the access road when she had exited the interstate on her way up to the Feldman residence. She decided to make a stop there on her way back, but first she needed to notify wildlife officials she spotted a mountain lion foraging the foothills.

* * * *

The service station attendant behind the counter was a chipper, college-age student with frizzled blond hair and a perpetual smile curled across his face.

"Yes, ma'am. I worked the graveyard shift, twelve to eight in the morning on New Year's Day. Now, here I am the day after working my normal eight to five. The schedule was out of whack last week because of the holidays. Some staff were off and others had to fill in wherever they could."

"What I'm trying to determine is whether two people we are looking for stopped in here early yesterday morning to service their car," Carlita said.

"What model car were they driving?" the attendant asked.

"A late model, white jeep. A hard top."

"You say two people were in it."

"Yes, a big burly man and an attractive, raven-haired woman of about the same age."

"Yes. They were here. I waited on them."

"Around what time, would you say?"

The attendant exhaled a deep breath and joggled his memory. "It was an early hour. I'd say close to one in the morning."

"Did you see which way they were headed when they left?"

"Nope. Another customer came to the counter right as they left."

"Do you have a security camera in operation here?"

"Yes we do."

"They filled up the tank?"

"Yes, to the top."

"Anything else you can tell me about them?"

"The woman used the restroom, if that's of any interest to you."

"She did? Where is it located?"

"Around the corner. We keep it locked overnight. They have to get a key from us to access it."

"When was the last time the cleaning crew was here?" she asked.

The attendant flashed a look of concern. "Does this place look that bad?" he asked.

"No. I was curious as to when the restrooms were last cleaned."

"Well, they don't work on holidays and they haven't been here yet today, so it's been nearly two days since they were last cleaned. I checked the rooms earlier and they're presentable, though."

"I'd like to see your women's restroom," she said.

"Help yourself. Like I said it's left unlocked during the day."

Carlita stepped around the corner to the women's room. It was empty, which was probably best for what she had in mind. She considered asking the attendant to put up the unavailable sign while she checked it but decided it was unnecessary.

The attendant was right. The facility was not altogether unpresentable. The sole eyesore was the handful of paper towels littering the floor from the overflowing disposal bins. The room contained twin washbasins and towel dispensers, in addition to the overflowing bins.

Carlita donned her gloves and went to work. She started with the right side bin, carefully digging her way through the discarded towels to the bottom, her burrowing resulting in additional towels on the floor. Finding nothing of import, she moved across to the companion bin. She had barely begun when a short, matronly-looking woman entered the room. The two exchanged apprehensive looks and went about their business—Carlita was bin diving and the customer was primping as fast as she could. Finished with her grooming, the woman hurriedly washed her hands and reached to snatch a towel from the dispenser, only to find it empty. Seeing her plight, Carlita snatched one from her side and handed it to the woman, who at once dried her hands and rushed out of the room. Meanwhile, Carlita had landed her hand on something hard near the bottom of the bin, something metallic, something wrapped in a towel unlike the ones in the restroom. She lifted the item from the container and unwrapped it on the washbasin counter. Laid out before her was a small kitchen knife, its blade stained with blood. She took the knife between her thumb and forefinger and raised it to the lights above to examine the stains. The instant she did, the woman who moments ago rushed out, reentered the room. Acting very unconcerned about the woman in uniform with the raised knife in her hand, she casually walked to the counter to retrieve the tiny purse she had left behind in her haste. Carlita gave her a bemused smile as the woman turned to leave.

Carlita rewrapped the knife in the same towel it came in, walked to the sheriff's car and placed it in an evidence bag. She subsequently contacted headquarters to tell them to get the forensics people back to the Feldman home. She next returned to the restroom to clean up her mess. On her way out, she thanked the service attendant for his cooperation and headed back to the Feldman residence to see if the towel and the knife matched up with what was in the house. Following that, she needed to contact Detective Jolly who was on the road to brief him on her findings.

Henry Hoffman

The forensics crew was already on hand at the Feldman residence when Carlita arrived for her second go-around. Her first stop after her arrival was the kitchen where, with gloved hands, she spread open the wrapped package on a counter. She then pulled a sample towel from a wall dispenser and held it against the piece of paper in which the knife was wrapped. They were a perfect match. She next opened a cutlery cabinet and withdrew one of the knives to match it against the bloodied instrument. They also were identical, save for the stains.

Carlita left the items in the care of the forensics people who were busy taking photographs of the scene. Satisfied with the results, she took the opportunity to conduct a quick check of the remainder of the house. To her mild surprise, it was as if a line of demarcation had been drawn down the center of the two bedroom, two bath home. One side could best be described as chaotic with its disheveled bedroom and messy bath, a sharp contrast to the orderly appearance of the opposite side. From the looks of things, Carlita surmised the inhabitants led separate lives, perhaps held together by the thread of a golden dream. There was no doubt which side belonged to whom. The question was, did it make a difference in the grand scheme of things? Did the old adage "where there is disorder there is chaos" apply in this case? Did the disorder, or for that matter the order, provide clues to each individual's state of mind? She also wondered what she should make of the fact that the two living arrangements were alike in one glaring respect: there was not a single personal photograph on display anywhere in the house. Did Daniela haul hers off with her other possessions? Was Arlen Feldman so devoid of personal relationships he had none to display? Could this be a sign of the depressing lives they were leading?

Carlita decided she was spinning a web of speculation and pop psychology, neither of which was her forte. She concluded she would stick to the hard evidence and let the prosecutors decide if the conjecture was worth pursuing. What was not in doubt was that it was past time for her to get in touch with Detective Jolly.

CHAPTER FIFTEEN

Jolly checked his watch. "Seven-thirty. On time."

A silence ensued as the sheriff's detective and Adam absorbed the events leading up to the chase. Minutes later, they reached the turnoff to the airport and Treetop Lodge. No sooner did they make the turn than the car lost traction for an instant, lurching into a sidespin until the detective managed to bring it back under control. "Black ice," he said. "The conditions are ripe for it."

"And those conditions are?" Adam, the warm weather guy, asked.

"A cold front passing through like this one freezes the melting snow. It's common in the early morning and difficult as hell to detect. You can usually spot it in the shaded areas of the road. Otherwise, you're at its mercy."

The road led them up a long incline at the top of which the airport came into view off to their left. Fronting the airfield was the facility's office, a half-pipe structure made of corrugated steel. It stood back a quarter of a mile or so from the highway. The sole other building on the premises was a hangar. A number of light planes, some tied to the ground, were scattered about. Surrounding the complex was a perimeter fence. A parking lot adjacent to the office was empty, save for one pickup truck.

Jolly eased the vehicle off the road and to a stop for a leisurely look.

"What make of car does Daniela drive?" Adam asked.

"Dark blue Chevy Impala...late model."

A lone truck rumbled past from the opposite direction, its driver casting a wary glance their way as though expecting a cop on his tail at any moment.

"Any reason we don't wait for them here?" Adam asked.

"It's best to get where they are," Jolly said, pulling the car back onto the road. "Despite what we may think, there's no guarantee they're headed here."

As they left the airport in their rear view, Adam was convinced it would soon be back in play again.

The dispatcher suddenly came on the radio, informing them he was patching in Detective Perez at her request.

"I thought it best to give you my report on the search right away," she said through the static.

"How'd it go?" Jolly asked.

"We've got the timeline firmed up thanks to a neighbor," she said. "Daniela and Fielding hooked up following the New Year's Eve festivities and made an early morning run in his jeep to pick up the gold. They left about one or one-thirty in the morning and returned around four or four-thirty, well before the stakeout came on duty. There were small clumps of dirt in the backseat of the jeep, similar to the ones we found in the Land Rover on the bridge. There was a confrontation either in the driveway or in the kitchen, but for what reason, we do not know. I found blood on some gravel rocks in their driveway close to Fielding's jeep. There's also blood in the kitchen. By the way, they must be traveling in Daniela's Chevy, since his vehicle was the only one here. I also was able to locate what I'm sure is the knife used in the attack. I located it in a trash bin at a nearby filling station. The service attendant said they stopped there in the early morning to fill the jeep's tank. It was a kitchen knife stained with blood and wrapped in a paper towel. The towel and knife both matched up with the towels and knives in the Feldman kitchen. They're both in the hands of forensics for examination. There are a few other details but I wanted to get this information to you as fast as I could. Oh, and one other item: I was able to contact the airport and alert them to the situation."

"Good work, Carlita," Jolly said. "That definitely narrows things down."

The sheriff's detective returned his attention to the road ahead. "Are you prepared for what lies ahead?" he asked out of the blue.

"For what lies ahead?" Adam repeated. "I'm not packing, if that's what you mean."

Jolly glanced down at the holstered gun beneath his opened jacket. "No. What I mean is, are you ready for the truth?"

"I'm always ready for the truth. You'll have to explain. I'm a slow learner," he said, a bit annoyed at the vague questioning.

"Thanks to Carlita we now have some hard evidence instead of a boatload of conjecture that Daniela and Fielding are involved in a crime, or at least accomplices to one. If so, who's to say Fielding is not the mastermind, the guy who jumped in to take over once he found out there was a pot of gold to be had. In my experience, things are rarely the way they seem when criminality is involved. The fact is, at the end of this road we're traveling the truth will come out in real time with you and I as witnesses. Whatever comes later is the filtered version, molded and shaped to their liking by lawyers on both sides."

They were traversing a second steep incline when they encountered more black ice. Jolly spun and lurched the car over one ice patch to another, utilizing the dry spots in between like stepping-stones to the top of the hill. "If this keeps up, this stuff will be forming into a solid coat before long," he said between efforts to control the vehicle. A few final twists and turns and they were back on the straight and narrow of a plateau, less than two miles from the Treetop Lodge, if Adam's calculations were correct.

As luck would have it, he would never find out if his calculations were right, for around the next bend appeared a dark blue sedan, closing fast in their direction. "Is this the one?" he asked.

"Yep, this looks like it," Jolly said.

There was instant recognition all around as the two cars passed. It was Daniela's car but it was Reggie at the wheel. Perhaps an indication of who was in charge, Adam thought, starting again with the speculation.

Jolly slowed the sheriff's car, executed a U-turn, flipped on the flashers and siren, and fishtailed the vehicle nearly off the road. The maneuver immediately launched Reggie into full flight.

They were running thirty yards behind the fleeing vehicle. Jolly contacted the dispatcher. "Looks like we may be needing backup," he said.

"Is that a request?" the dispatcher asked.

"Yes. It's a request. We're about five miles from the airport, approaching from the north."

"No way are they still using the airport as an escape route now," Adam said above the wail of the siren.

"Agreed. What we can't do, however, is let them out of our sight. We give them time to ditch that gold again and we're pretty much back where we started."

When they approached the long dip in the road they'd climbed minutes earlier, Jolly closed to within twenty yards of the Chevy. Viewing it from the top, Adam likened it to an Olympic ski-jump slope, a steep plunge of slippery pathway with a short incline in the middle and ending in a flat stretch at the bottom. The problem was, as a roadside sign warned, the level base veered sharply to the right though a cut hill.

"What do you say, Fraley? Is conducting a chase in these conditions worth the risk?" Jolly asked. "After all, they're not likely to escape the perimeter."

"What is that stock reply teenagers give when warned of the dangers of smoking?" Adam asked in return. "You've got to die of something."

"Hold on then," Jolly said, as they began their descent.

It quickly became apparent there would be no weaving from one ice patch to another on this run. The black ice had taken complete command of the road, at once sending both vehicles out of control. No amount of skillful steering wheel maneuvering or brake manipulation would wrest control back.

"Have you ever considered a move to Florida?" Adam asked, bracing a hand against the dashboard.

"In moments like this? Of course," Jolly said between furious twists of the wheel. "Can't beat the views here, though, can you?" he cracked.

"Thank God there's no other traffic," Adam said, finding a kernel of hope in their predicament.

"Nobody else is dumb enough to be driving in these conditions," Jolly said in frustration, unable to gain traction to right the vehicle. "We might as well be driving on donut wheels."

They may not have been gaining traction, but they were holding speed, running over fifty miles per hour by Adam's estimation despite traveling much of the distance sideways. Up ahead, Reggie was matching them twist for twist, lurch for lurch, and spin for spin. Awaiting them at the bottom was the cut hill, backstopping the bend of the highway.

"Remember what I said about learning the truth in moments like this," Jolly said, delivering his final instruction.

Reggie slammed into the slabs of exposed rock that formed the backstop split seconds before them, skidding across the road and into the hill's face, broadsiding it on the driver's side of the vehicle. Jolly followed, managing to avoid the Chevy but not the rock face, ramming into it after a final spin on the ice.

Moments later, echoes of screeching tires and a wailing siren no longer reverberated through the hills. Filling the void was the blare of a stuck horn and the hiss of a busted radiator.

"Backup may be delayed due to driving conditions," crackled the dispatcher's voice through a shattered window.

* * * *

The horn and hiss subsided, bringing a momentary quiet to the scene. Black and white images flickered before Adam's eyes like scenes from a silent movie. Once again, he found himself peering over the side of the Royal Gorge Bridge into the depths below but this time to a far different scene. A Spanish galleon, fitted with eight large wooden wheels under its hull, had been converted into an amphibian vessel and had made its way up the Arkansas River. It was moored to two electrical power posts. The ship's gangplanks were lowered to the ground, up and down which crewmen streamed to and from the adjacent hills hauling sacks of gold back to the mother ship like an army of ants. Suddenly, into the scene roared a steam engine, belching a towering column of black smoke. It was pulling four coal cars filled with sheriff's deputies instead of the usual mineral. No sooner had the train come to a halt than

145

the galleon let loose a broadside from its multi-decks of guns, derailing two of the coal cars. "Time to put our plan into action," he could hear Jolly say in a voice that sounded like it was coming from the North Pole. "Fraley...Fraley. Can you hear me? Time to put our plan into action!"

Adam felt a hand nudging his shoulder, awakening him from his reverie. He rolled his body from its slumped position and took quick measure of the situation. He then shoved open the sheriff's car door, grabbed hold of Jolly slumped behind the steering wheel and dragged him across the front seat toward the passenger side door. He had him halfway out the door when Daniela jumped from the Chevy and, limping badly, made a beeline for the sheriff's car. "He made me do it!" she shouted breathlessly, one arm flailing about, the other pointing back at her car. "You need to stop him!"

The Chevy's driver side door swung open and Reggie stumbled out, nearly tripping to the ground. Regaining his balance, he plodded determinedly toward them. His forehead was bloodied, though the remainder of his imposing frame looked intact. He appeared the menacing ogre Adam could never have imagined.

"Stop him!" Daniela yelled, the fire in her eyes intense enough to burn holes in the black ice. "He's gone crazy. He'll kill us all."

Running out of time, Adam managed to free one arm from under Jolly and reached inside the detective's jacket to remove his revolver from its holster. "Here, hold this on him until I get this guy out of the car. She took the weapon, grabbed it with both hands and aimed it at the oncoming Reggie, halting him in his tracks.

Adam finished dragging Jolly from the car and propped him up against the front wheel.

"What's wrong with him?" Daniela called out, keeping one eye on Reggie.

"Not sure. Knocked out maybe. Looks like he's coming around."

Adam stood to confront his former Air Force colleague who was displaying a very calm exterior for someone having a gun pointed at him by a stoked woman. No exchange of words was necessary for Adam to understand what had transpired between him and Reggie. They had become strangers overnight, the façade of friendship collapsed by time and circumstance.

Reggie was the first to break off eye contact, turning to Daniela with a resolve in his eyes, as if to say, "It's your move."

Daniela shuffled her feet side-to-side in an overt display of indecision, much like a panicky squirrel before an oncoming truck. In one final movement, she tightened her grip on the revolver and swung it directly at the face of Adam.

For the first time in his life, Adam was looking down the barrel of a gun. Above the barrel Daniela's eyes were peering determinedly back at him. She blinked them once, twice, three times, and then pulled the trigger.

Click.

She pulled it a second and third time.

Click...click.

"Whose side are you on now, Daniela?" Adam asked.

"You stupid bitch," Reggie said.

"Good thing you remembered to take the right revolver and not this one," Jolly said, slipping a second pistol from an ankle holster and rising to his feet as though by miracle.

Daniela tossed the empty weapon at them and buried her face in her hands.

"Check the car's interior and trunk," Jolly instructed Adam. "The keys I assume are still in the ignition."

Adam retrieved the keys and checked inside the vehicle, only to discover a couple of suitcases crammed with clothes, along with two personal traveling kits. It was with far greater expectation he next popped open the trunk. Much to his surprise, he found it empty, except for a shovel, its scoop clean of debris.

"Looks like we've got a shell game going on here," Jolly said to the assembled.

"Need I say you've got nothing," Reggie remarked from a distance.

"How about attempted murder, for starters?" Jolly retorted.

"That's your story," Reggie replied. "All we were attempting to do was go on a vacation. That was until you mistakenly took us for criminals and ran us off the road."

Jolly turned his attention to Adam. "Any broken bones?"

"As best I can tell, they're all still in one piece. How about you?"

147

"Same."

The backups arrived. They confiscated the Chevy, and took Daniela and Reggie into custody after reading them their rights. They then checked the condition of the damaged sheriff's car and deemed it in a workable state for the time being, despite a couple of bad body dents. Unlike the car, the condition of the road had improved considerably. The rising sun was beaming down in greater force, burning off the black ice in amounts sufficient to entice a trickle of traffic back to the road. Minutes later Jolly and Adam joined the trickle, heading south toward Highway 50.

"You were expecting to see Fielding's footlocker full of gold in the trunk?" Jolly asked from behind the wheel.

"Don't tell me you weren't," Adam said. "I would have bet my pickup on it."

"What did the shovel tell you?"

"Pretty apparent to me. They were on their way to dig up the loot."

"Too bad we weren't tailing them instead of chasing them," Jolly said.

"You're not serious about throwing an attempted murder charge at them, are you? I doubt it would fly."

"It gives them something to think about," Jolly said. "Obviously, the prosecutor's office will have the final say on it. To tell you the truth, I'm more concerned with closing the Rita Feldman case. Let's face it. The motive behind all of this still eludes us, hidden who knows where."

Up ahead, the airport came into view. "Can we make a quick stop here?" Adam asked. "I have a question for the manager."

Jolly swung the car onto the access road leading to the complex's parking lot. Four cars occupied slots adjacent to the office building. Jolly made it five. Out on the airstrip a light plane was taxiing for takeoff. Inside, a husky, baldheaded man with a finely trimmed goatee stood behind a service counter. Jolly identified himself and Adam.

"Stan Corrigan," he said, extending a hand to both. "Yeah, a lady from your office called earlier today and asked us to nix a scheduled flight. Can't recall that ever happening."

"Can you tell us what time the flight was scheduled to leave?" Adam asked.

Corrigan reached under the counter and pulled out a logbook. He flipped it open and ran his finger to the bottom of the page before stopping on an entry. "Eleven this morning."

"Are there storage bins on the premises?" Jolly asked.

Corrigan shook his head. "Most load their stuff the day they're scheduled for takeoff, that's if they're carrying cargo to begin with."

Jolly thanked the man and along with Adam headed for the door. "By the way," Corrigan called out to them, "what do I tell those people if they show up at eleven?"

"They won't," Jolly called back, as the two exited the building.

"Okay, what did we learn?" Jolly asked on their walk to the car. "I assumed you had something other than a restroom break in mind for wanting to stop here."

"We learned they were scheduled to leave at eleven. That means they had approximately a two-hour window to retrieve the gold and make it back in time for their scheduled departure."

"Meaning the gold is located relatively close by," Jolly said.

"Yes and not a great distance away at all," Adam responded.

"You say that as though you know exactly where it's buried. Is that why you brought their shovel along?"

"Yes, I know precisely where it's buried," Adam said, as they reached the car.

Jolly leaned an arm on the side of the vehicle and looked across the top of it at his volunteer. "Care to share?"

"It's buried where it's always been buried."

* * * *

Jolly followed the route to the Royal Gorge Bridge, traversing it with none of the drama of the previous day's crossing. No falling bodies to distract from the view, Adam mused. Moreover, they were not in need of the map, the pathway still fresh in their minds.

The brown patch of ground appeared no different from the first time they observed it, save for the one major difference buried beneath it, Adam reckoned. He wasted no time taking the shovel from the car and scooping the dirt out.

149

"At least the turf remains soft for digging," Jolly observed from the sideline, drawing a wan smile from Adam. "What makes you think they didn't rebury it overnight?" he asked.

"The shovel's blade was whistle clean," Adam replied. "No, it was here all the time."

"How stupid of us not to have asked ourselves why they refilled the hole," Jolly lamented.

"What's not stupid is that mistakes happen," Adam said. "How often do we discover later in an investigation the answer was always right in front of us, or in this instance below us?"

Four feet down Adam struck metal. Hurriedly, he scooped dirt from over and around the object, instantly recognizing it for what it was: Reggie's footlocker. Completing the excavation, he grabbed one of the side leather handles and Jolly the other. Together they lifted the trunk from its burial place and onto the surface.

"Nice for us he had that RF engraved on there," Jolly said, taking a step back from the locker. "Do you want to do the honors?" he went on to ask, handing Adam his pair of gloves.

Adam donned the gloves, leaned down to unsnap the latch, and lifted the lid. At once images of sunken Spanish galleons and pirate ships danced in his head as he observed what lay before him. The word "treasure" took on an entirely new meaning for him now that he was viewing it in the flesh. The locker was filled to the brim with glittering gold coins of all sizes, a hoard equivalent to a Cripple Creek mini mother lode. Several of the coins slipped from the container onto the loose dirt. Adam reached down to retrieve them, wiping them of debris. When finished, he exchanged a quick smile of satisfaction with Jolly before returning them to the footlocker.

"There's your motive," Adam said.

Jolly nodded, his eyes affixed to the haul. "I'd say it qualifies as one."

"Daniela and Reggie didn't retrieve the gold on their early morning run," Adam said. "They transferred it to the footlocker and left it buried here."

"For logistics purposes," Jolly said.

"Right. They wanted it close by when they made their run. They were committed to an escape by air but needed a day of pre-flight preparation or else they would have taken the gold back with them on their early morning run."

"And that's what led to the confrontation."

"Correct," Adam said. "Arlen Feldman had to be worrying where his wife was at that early hour and on the lookout for her return. When they arrived home, he caught them in the act of unloading the empty chest to transfer it to his car. Doubtless, she had a key to his Land Rover. That's when the fireworks erupted."

"Yeah, it was a gamble on their part the gold would not be disturbed. They figured right. In our rush, we had no reason to doubt the grab and go had been executed. The evidence was right there in front of us," Jolly said.

"Yep. Like we conjectured at the time, they placed the empty chest into the Land Rover's trunk to muddy the waters."

Adam handed the gloves back to Jolly who slipped them on. "Take one last look. You may never see anything as valuable as this again in your lifetime," he said, taking a moment to let them absorb the sight before reaching down to close the container.

"I've already seen something as valuable as this on my trip," Adam said, leaving a puzzled look on the sheriff detective's face.

CHAPTER SIXTEEN

"An appraiser the department brought in estimates the value of the haul at close to seven figures, give or take a few thousand," Jolly revealed to Adam at a post-investigation conference between the two.

"Whose hands do you suppose it will end up in?" Adam asked.

"The DA's hoping they can get it back in the hands of Arlen Feldman's victims."

"Any word on what charges might be filed?"

"Charges are pending all the way around, though Daniela already has admitted to prosecutors Arlen Feldman's claim of being home on Christmas Eve was bogus. He was gone for a good portion of the evening. Daniela claims she thought it was to visit his child. Still, charges against him are unlikely. A defendant has the right to face his accusers and since he's no longer with us, it becomes a moot point. Occasionally, there is a judicial inquiry in situations like this to determine compensation to victims. In this case, you can bet your bottom dollar there'll be a flood of claims. You want to put yours in?" Jolly jested.

"Based on what? A finders-keepers claim? I doubt that argument will hold water," Adam said. "Besides, I feel fortunate in escaping any share of the blame."

"You have anything you want to say to Fielding?" Jolly asked.

"Nothing," Adam said. "Oh sure, I'd like to ask him exactly when it was he decided to cross to the dark side and whether it was in fact my gold-hoarding theory that ultimately shoved him in that direction. But no, the look on his face the moment Daniela pulled the trigger told me all I needed to know about our relationship. The bullet may have been a phantom one, but it put an end to whatever friendship existed. Maybe someday down the line I'll be in a forgiving mood, but not now. I'm no Prospero."

"Who's Prospero?"

"Some guy who was exiled by an evil brother and king to a deserted island with his daughter. He ended up being the forgiving type."

"In all likelihood you wouldn't be able to speak to Fielding before the trial anyway. I'm sure the defense attorneys would not be keen on the idea, since anything said in a jailhouse interview is considered fair game for prosecutors."

"As I said, down the line I may reconsider it."

"You got all your belongings out of his condo?"

"Yes. I'm officially out of there. I'm holing up in a motel room until that unfinished business we spoke of is completed," Adam said. "Have you heard anything from Carlita regarding it?"

"She's setting up a meeting for tomorrow morning."

"How much work is there left for her to do?"

"I know she's completed the background check on you. A thorough one, I might add," Jolly said with a smile.

"How thorough?"

"What do you want to know about yourself?"

"That thorough, huh?"

"Carlita is compulsive when it comes to collecting details on a person's past. Not much escapes her. "Past is prologue," she keeps saying, especially when it comes to predicting a person's behavior."

"What are my chances?" Adam asked.

"You've got her on your side. That's a big plus. She knows who the decision makers are in the childcare system and they know her. She works closely with them. As you no doubt know, kids often end up as collateral damage in criminal cases. When that happens, she by choice becomes the child's advocate. She herself has been a foster mother."

"The meeting is across the street at the state office building?" Adam asked.

"Yep. Nine in the morning," Jolly said. "One piece of advice: get a second opinion before you make your final decision."

"I plan on speaking to my former boss the minute I get back to the motel."

"Pete Peterson?"

"Yes. How did you know?"

"I told you Carlita was compulsive."

"Pete still serves as my mentor in and out of the profession. That's the way it works in a compact work environment like ours: small office, small separation, before and after."

"Like family," Jolly said.

"Like family," Adam repeated, which reminded him he also had best consult with his parents. If anyone knew of the trials and tribulations of the trail he was about to embark on, it would be them.

* * * *

"What's the problem? Not enough crime in Florida to keep you busy, so you had to go looking for it elsewhere?" his former boss asked.

"Happenstance...it happens everywhere," Adam replied.

"Some sheriff's gal from up there called me yesterday. Said she was doing a background check on you but was vague as hell as to what it was all about. I asked to speak to her supervisor to find out if she was legit and she was. She proceeded to grill me for everything I knew about you. I even called Tamra to find out if she knew what it was all about. She said she got the same call and same grilling but didn't know what was going on. She thought maybe it had to do with a case you got involved in up there in Colorado. So, what's up? You're not looking for a new job, are you?"

"No, not at all. What it's all about is a personal relationship. On the advice of another wise old bird up here, that's what I'm looking for from you—a second opinion."

The revelation prompted an audible chuckle on the other end of the line. "You need a second opinion for that?"

"Yes."

"Must be the sheriff's daughter, if he has one," Peterson said. "It's the male-female kind, I take it."

154

"Yes, again."

"I suppose you're going to tell me she's beautiful beyond words or something of the sort."

"Yes, beautiful beyond words."

"Is she smart?"

"Very smart."

"We're not talking about Tamra, are we? You once said she might be the ultimate test for you to not cross the personal-professional line."

"It's not Tamra."

"Let's see. You've had one relationship with an older woman and a potential one with a woman your age in Tamra," Peterson said. "I'm betting we're going younger this time."

"A good bet."

"How old dare I ask?"

"Seven."

Silence on the other end.

"Going on seven-and-a-half," Adam added.

More silence.

"Seriously, Pete. Let me explain. You know how I value your opinion. You've never let me down with your advice and I'm not about to go against it now."

"Explain then."

* * * *

Carlita was waiting for him in the hallway outside the meeting room door. "How goes it?" Adam asked her.

"So far, so good," she said, clutching a large notebook against her chest. "The big thing we have going for us is that all states have signed onto the I.C.P.S., which means state lines can now be crossed."

"What's that?" Jolly asked, having joined them, a power drink in hand.

"The Interstate Compact for the Placement of Children," she replied.

"Anything else we got going for us?" Adam asked.

"Carlita, for one thing," Jolly chimed in, warming to the occasion.

"How desperate the need is always a consideration," she said. "Mostly, it boils down to the applicant and key decision makers."

"As I told you, she knows them all," Jolly interjected, drawing a what-can-I-say shrug from his partner. In this matter, the veteran detective was leaving no doubt he had full confidence in her.

"Is she in there?" Adam asked, motioning to the room.

"Yes, and by the way, she's writing a letter to you," Carlita replied.

They entered from the rear of the small room set up in classroom style. Carlita and Jolly slipped silently in into a couple of chairs within earshot of the room's front. Located at the head of the room were a table and three chairs. One chair faced the rear of the room. A second positioned at the far end of the rectangular table was occupied by the matronly woman from Children's Services. A third facing the front of the room was occupied by Noelle. Pen in hand, she had the left side of her face nearly flat against the table's surface, eyeing intently from a side angle her careful stroking of the pen on a piece of stationery.

"Hello Noelle," Adam said, sliding into the chair across from her.

Instantly, she lifted her head and widened her eyes in surprise.

"How are you?" he asked, his heart thumping in his ears.

"Okay," she said, squeezing her shoulders together. "I told them you'd be back."

"And here I am. Is that a letter you're writing?"

"Yes. I'm almost finished," she said, glancing down at her work.

"Is it for me?"

She nodded. "When are you going home?"

"Very soon," he said, drawing his chair closer to the table. "Noelle, do you remember the story I told you on Christmas Eve? The one about the man and his daughter stuck on a deserted island?"

"Yes, I remember," she said. "The magic story."

"Don't you sort of feel like you've been deserted--stuck on an island you can't get off of?"

"Yes, but I don't have any magic to get me off."

"Oh, but you do have magic in you, more than you'll ever know." Adam said. He leaned in closer. "I have a question for you."

She tightened her shoulders once more in youthful anticipation.

"How would you like to come to Florida?"

Her eyes lit up. "For how long?" she asked.

"For how long?" The answer came easy to Adam. "How about forever?"

Noelle glanced at the Children's Services representative. Adam could have sworn he saw a hint of a smile on the woman's face.

"Who would I stay with?" Noelle asked.

"You'd stay with me," Adam said.

"You'd have to take me to church every Sunday."

"I can do that."

Adam could feel the emotions stirring in her as if they were his very own. "Is that a yes I see in your eyes?"

"Yes," she said, bobbing her head vigorously.

He pulled a small packet from his shirt pocket and held it in front of her. "This is a return trip ticket I bought yesterday. I will be coming back to see you in less than a month. Carlita, the lady sitting in the back of the room, who I believe you know very well, will explain everything and keep in touch with you until I return."

Noelle swiveled in her seat and gave a wave to Carlita before returning her attention to Adam. "You promise to come back?"

"I promise," he said. "Didn't I promise to come back last time?"

She nodded. "You won't get lost this time, will you?"

"No, I won't get lost."

Adam pointed to the piece of stationery in front of her on the table. "Don't forget to finish this letter. I'm looking forward to reading it when I get back home."

"I will," she said.

Adam took her hand in his. "Listen, I have to go now. Remember, it won't be long before I'll be back."

She again nodded vigorously.

"Do I get a hug?" he asked, releasing her hand.

Noelle hopped from her chair and met him halfway around the table, throwing her arms around him. "Don't forget to finish that letter," he said.

"I won't. I'll mail it today," she said. "Will you write one too?"

"You bet," he said, motioning her back to the table. Turning to leave, he glanced over his shoulder to see her busily working the pen.

"Make it happen," he said to Carlita in the hallway.

"I'll do my best," she said. "There are still visits from social workers here and in Florida to be conducted, not to mention physicals and more background checks. There's also plenty of paperwork to complete. I'm thinking foster care to adoption is the most viable course to pursue." Carlita paused, folded her arms, and smiled. "As I said, Adam, it looks promising."

"Don't forget. You'll no doubt be getting a batch of depositions to sign," Jolly added. "If your testimony is required, you may have an additional trip to make, though I'm told a plea agreement between prosecutors, Daniela, and Fielding is already in the works. Both of the accused are being cooperative."

"I'm hoping for the extra trip," he said.

Adam bid his goodbyes to the two detectives, now fast friends if there ever were ones. An hour later, he was on the highway headed east, coming down from his Rocky Mountain high, or so he thought. The euphoria, it turned out, hung with him for miles on end, making his long cross-country journey seemingly a swift one. Now, if only good fortune remained by his side, there would be a letter awaiting him on his arrival home.

About the Author

Henry Hoffman is a former newspaper editor and public library director whose works have appeared in a variety of literary and trade publications, including the Library Journal, the Midwesterner, Encyclopedia of Library Science, America: History and Life, Historical Abstracts of the United States, the Cyclopedia of Literary Places, and the Encyclopedia of Natural Disasters. He is the author of five previous novels, including Bridge to Oblivion and The Veiled Lagoon, the first two entries in the Adam Fraley mystery series. He is the recipient of the Florida Publishers Association's Gold Medal Award for Florida Fiction.

Author Contact:

www.henryhoffman.net